Dragon Storm

Season of The Dragon

Book 2

J.E. Taylor

Cover Art by Joolz & Jarling

DRAGON STORM

My goal: make the last dragon rue the day he crossed me.

When the monsters broke their deal for humanity's surrender, the last dragon saved me from certain death. Unfortunately, Mikhail St. Clare played me like a professional grifter, making me think he was on our side, and not aligned with the Serpent King, who wants to stomp out humans like we were pesky insects.

Mikhail's special power to shift into human form aided his infiltration of my defenses, and ultimately coerced me into revealing my secret weapon against the monsters.

Then I stupidly led him right to our headquarters. I should have known. He was a dragon, after all. One that had facilitated the destruction of our ability to fight back on any mass scale against the Serpent King and his army of leviathans.

With nothing left to defend, I'm on a mission to make that bastard pay for what he has done.

But before I can find him and put a bullet in his brain, I have to cross a leviathan-patrolled city where every corner hides a hideous death.

1

I stared out my window at the raging river. It seemed to capture my turbulent mood accurately. The setting sun sent prisms of light off the chaotic waters, and I turned away from the stormy view. Too many monsters lived under the surface to have calm seas. It was as if they knew the last dragon had fled the city and they could not follow to drag him down into the deep to his death.

Mikhail St. Clare.

Savior.

Traitor.

Monster.

There were so many other words to describe him, and each one sent a twinge of fiery fury through me. He had told me he was the last dragon, but after his betrayal, I couldn't trust a thing he had said.

But I did know where his hideout was. He had his very own safe house here in the city, near the Brooklyn Bridge. The shit thing about being on the west side perpendicular to Central Park was the sheer distance the bridge was from where I stood.

And between me and my goal was an army of leviathans.

As much as I wanted to just curl up and ignore the rest of the world, I couldn't. I hadn't laid down to die when the monsters came, or when they declared war on humanity, and I certainly wasn't going to give up because I had been duped by a dragon. My grim stubbornness kicked into overdrive and I was now much more determined to wipe them off the map.

I had a goal: come leviathan or Serpent King, I would blast through anyone who got in my way just to get my hands around Mik St. Clare's throat.

He was mine to extinguish, and I would fight all the monsters to let my revenge loose.

I turned and stalked out of my apartment. I was all piss and vinegar until I got to the stairs. Walking down the steps reminded me of all my injuries sustained over the last few weeks in an excruciating crescendo.

Taking stock of my ailments brought a wince with each step. The backpack irritated the healing burn scabs on my back. Holding the railing was tough with the wrist puncture wounds from the shackles that had held me hostage so the leviathans could tear me to pieces.

If it hadn't been for Mikhail... I stanched the thought before it could fully form. Mik St. Clare was not a man to admire *or* desire. He was a dragon with the magical ability to shift. I forced the thought of him out of my head and focused on the stairs in front of me, cursing Mik under my breath with each painful step.

If he hadn't whisked you away from Grand Central Station, you may have been able to truly broker our surrender.

I stopped.

Did I really believe that? Had Mikhail somehow orchestrated the failure of our negotiations, or had he at least been telling the truth about the dark intentions of the Serpent King?

My thoughts swarmed, keeping me frozen in indecision. I forcefully shook Mikhail from my head. I'd drill him for information before I dealt the mortal blow. But for now, I had to get to his building shrouded in destruction before I could extract the truth from the bastard.

The only thoughts I would allow would be those that relished his violent end. He had torched the Museum of Natural History, where my platoon gathered. It did not matter that the commander had sentenced me to death alongside Mik. What mattered was Mik killed them all, and the dust of the dead swirled on the air, choking those near the epicenter of destruction.

He vaporized our only defense against the leviathans.

Our stockpile of bleach was as gone as everything else in the path of his raging fire. Now we would have to scrape and scratch for every available container of what was the equivalent of liquid gold. The pandemic depleted our reserves to begin with. Everyone panic-bought bleach, believing it would kill the virus. Nothing, not even the sterilization properties of bleach, killed the virus.

That motherfucker just had to die out on its own, along with half of humanity.

Then came the monsters from wherever they had been hibernating. And our numbers have been dwindling since they arrived. We were truly at their mercy. And the creatures did not have merciful bones in their disgustingly vile bodies.

Without bleach to penetrate the leviathans'
iron skin, we were a doomed species. Mikhail
toasting our massive stockpile, a stockpile *we*
hand delivered to my base, made his duplicity all
the more painful.

2

It took me much longer to climb down three flights of stairs than it should have, and by the time I reached the ground floor, my injuries sapped my energy. I leaned against the wall next to the door leading out to the street, second-guessing my plan. I was not sure I would make it down the length of the island of Manhattan.

One glance in the direction of Mikhail's path of destruction gave me a second wind. I had to see the damage firsthand. Hopefully, it would add to my dwindling reserve of strength and give me another blast of adrenaline to get me moving. The silence of the city struck me. What once was a bustling mecca now stood like a sepulcher. My footfalls on the blacktop echoed enough to keep my head turning and my muscles tense as I waited for predators to slink out of the dust and shadows. The tunnels provided darkness and stealth, but out here on the streets, the city that used to never sleep remained catatonic.

It was creepy on most days, but we were also running for our lives from the monsters, so really hearing the stillness made me pause. Even the river roiling behind me didn't break the quiet settling over Manhattan. Not even the footsteps of the monsters reached my ears.

"Damn," I whispered, just to make sure I had not somehow lost my hearing. My voice fell in a dive that hit the pavement, driving my steps forward. Two blocks away from the museum, the destruction started. One moment, I was in between the buildings and then, nothing. A desolate, dust-ridden scar broke the street, swallowing up everything in its path. Beyond the park, the scorching veered to the right, bypassing the park, and heading south, southeast. I couldn't see where it ended but it was a longer path than I had formerly thought. I swallowed hard.

The other platoons were farther south.

Could he have destroyed them, too?

That ominous thought quickened my pace and my heart. I kept a few feet from the edges of where Mikhail raked his fire over the land as the earth still radiated heat as if I stood next to a living lava flow.

I glanced at the smoldering path and picked up a small piece of metal debris from the road, tossing it into the scar. The metal bubbled and burst into flames.

Well, there goes a potential escape path.

If a leviathan came from the downtown direction, I had nowhere to run. Yet another reason to curse Mikhail St. Clare. Damn that dragon. I would make him pay for every slight, even if he could turn me to dust in an instant. I'd make sure I took him with me straight to the gates of hell.

The ash in the air made me cough, and my mind kept circling around what I might be inhaling. After all, when the towers came down that awful day in September of 2001, the dust from that caused cancer in survivors who were closest to Ground Zero. I rummaged in the depths of my inside pocket of my coat and pulled out a cloth mask, as if I were producing a rabbit out of a hat. Leave it to me to keep one of these silly things shoved in my pocket. But I was glad I had been diligent on the mask wearing protocol, even though I thought it was crazy and really did nothing in the height of the pandemic.

I slipped the mask on, praying it was enough to filter out the dust so I could avoid a debilitating disease later in life, assuming I lived long enough. Especially with the deadly trek I was currently on. Maybe the dragon was right. Maybe I did have a death wish. But, right now, an anger burning hotter than the scorched earth drove me forward.

I kept an eye in the downtown direction, but nothing stirred. It was as if Mikhail's actions silenced the monsters. His fiery scar stretched across the park and as I made my way around the pond, to the far corner where we had been left for dead, I blinked at the absence of the statue that we had been chained to. He destroyed it along with some of the buildings on Fifth Avenue. But the Plaza Hotel was left untouched.

The skyline of this area of the city had been transformed. I don't ever remember being able to see the Chrysler Building sparkling above the dust cloud like a beacon from this specific point at the edge of the park. It was usually hidden from view by the MetLife Building. But the path to it was clear now.

My heart leapt into my throat and instead of a brisk walk, I put on some speed despite my body's protests. It took me fifteen minutes at a light jog to reach the destination that had my pulse pounding. I stopped and stared at where Grand Central Station had been, almost in the same spot I had stood weeks ago to negotiate for our lives. But all that was left was half the hotel, and beyond the station the Chrysler Building towered untouched by dragon fire.

Mikhail had destroyed the monsters' home base and probably all the subway paths for miles. I shivered and glanced around. I was exposed standing here, just gawking. My mind could not grasp how far his fire could have gone underground. Especially with the sheer destruction topside.

God, I hope no one was down there.

But even as the thought formed, I already knew their fate. They would have never known what hit them. If I had to choose a death, that would be much preferred to being toyed with or torn to pieces a little bit at a time while the monsters laughed at your pain.

My head turned toward downtown. I needed to get to Mikhail's hideaway and confront him. I needed to know why before I plunged a knife into his chest.

3

I made it to the beginning of Union Square before I felt the first disturbance on the ground. The subway entrance was too far from where I stood to make a break for it. I pulled my spray bottle of bleach from the holder on the side of my backpack and held it at the ready. Unfortunately, I would have to let the damn monster get close in order to douse it. The spray bottle did not have the distance of a super-soaker.

A ball of fear formed at the back of my throat, constricting my chest. I gulped it down, forcing myself to take long, slow breaths despite the pounding of my heart. One swipe of the leviathan's claws could slice me in half, especially if I stayed out here in the road. I slid into the park and found a tree that was wide enough to hide me from view. I contemplated climbing it, but the leaves had all shed and I would be as easy to pick as a piece of meat from a shish kebab.

A shiver climbed up my spine as the ground rumbled again. This time the vibrations were closer than before, but I could not tell the direction it came from. I scanned the city toward the downtown area from around the tree, even looking behind me from the direction of the devastation Mikhail had left. Although I didn't think that was the direction they came from, I couldn't tell. It was as unspecific as pinpointing the direction an earthquake came from while you were in the midst of it.

I pulled my hood up over my head and sprayed the back of it along with my backpack and down to my pants and shoes. If there were more than one, I did not want them to get a whiff of me. But if they already had, very little would deter them. They would search me out like a cat stalking a mouse.

With a deep breath, I glanced around the tree and froze. The Serpent King slithered up Broadway with the army of leviathans marching behind him. The closest I had ever been to the Serpent King had been from the window of Mikhail's safe house. But being at street level made my body tense hard enough to almost squeeze the piss out of my bladder. I crouched down closer to the ground in an attempt to make myself invisible.

But as they marched by, nearly half a football field away from where I crouched, I saw what they dragged behind the Serpent King. My heart stopped for a moment at the chained dragon. Its wings were shredded, as if the entire leviathan army had a swipe at them. They flew in tattered bloody pieces, but he was alive, despite the damage.

The dragon's nostrils flared, and Mikhail's citrine eyes flashed my way as they passed, as though he knew I hid among the trees. If there had been foliage, I would have been well hidden, but even with my crouching in the leaves, I knew he saw me. Yet, he did not alert the army to my presence. He just turned his head back in the direction they were dragging him.

I stayed down until the last of the procession passed. Then I looked toward the downtown area. Toward Mikhail's safe house, remembering what they had done to his friend. They made a spectacle of killing him and then dragging his dead body through the streets as a warning.

My hands clenched as tight as my teeth at the thought of Mikhail's dead body being dragged through Manhattan in the same manner. It burned in a way I did not expect. I wanted revenge, at my hands. I did not want the monsters to kill him for me.

I turned and sprinted, cursing my slow pace and my screaming injuries. If I ran headlong into a leviathan, I was prepared to do as much damage as possible. But they were not doing their grid rotations. Instead, they stayed on course. I made it to a side street near Times Square in time to see a leviathan pound a stake into the ground. The stake held the iron chain that ended around Mikhail's throat.

When they stepped away from the damaged dragon, the Serpent King's gravelly voice echoed through the silence, loud enough to be heard for blocks. "I give you an offering. The one who disrupted our peace treaty and left the path of destruction across your city is yours to deal with. We will not intercede."

I stared from my hiding place, watching in horrified fascination as the monsters withdrew down Broadway and then dispersed out of view. I crept forward, wondering what type of trick this was. The monsters seemed to relish our cries of terror and pain just before they snuffed out our lives, so this did not feel right.

As much as I did not trust Mikhail, I couldn't help but hear the Serpent King's same rasping voice proclaiming his true intentions of wiping us all out.

Did Mikhail have the equipment to fabricate a recording?

The thought scraped at my skin, making it itch and ripple like it wanted to retreat inside me. I glanced at the dragon, wondering whether anything he told me had been true. A flare of hot pain struck through my chest, as if an evil cupid had pierced me with a bitter arrow.

When the last of the leviathans had slunk out of view, I moved forward with my spray bottle still in one hand and my revolver in the other. I wasn't the only one approaching Mikhail St. Clare, either. Soldiers came from the direction of the nearest subway entrance, pointing weapons at Mikhail.

And the dragon's chest turned red.

I sprinted forward, holding both weapons in the air. "Don't!" I yelled. I wasn't sure whether my command was for Mikhail to not unleash his fire, or for the people not to harm the dragon.

I was conflicted at seeing him so vulnerable. Plus, I had too many questions that needed answers before I'd allow anyone to kill him.

Mikhail's chest was orange now as if he held in the rising flames. "Run, Holly," he hissed at me.

I slid to a stop a few feet to his right unfazed by the troops surrounding us. I pointed my gun at Mikhail, letting my fury surface. "Why?" I growled through my teeth.

"Because you are in grave danger." He looked to the south.

"No, you insensitive idiot. Why the hell did you destroy our only chance?" I snarled. "Why did you kill my entire platoon?"

"For the love of everything sacred, run. Now," he hissed louder.

Mikhail's voice was so full of pain and urgency that I finally registered what was happening around us. Others approached the dragon with their weapons drawn as well, except they were not facing Mikhail anymore like they had been when I first ran out into the square. The soldiers faced the streets to the south, east, and west.

Leviathans stood with their mouths salivating at every street entrance surrounding us. A few blocks down Broadway, the Serpent King came back into view with a smug look on his reptilian face, as though we had walked willingly into their all-you-can-eat buffet.

And we were the main course.

At least there were only a half-dozen leviathans as opposed to the entire army of them, so those of us gathered around Mikhail might have a chance to get out of this alive.

But it still made my mouth run dry and my palms sweat.

I traded looks with the soldiers surrounding me. They had heard the dragon call me by name. They had heard the warning. Although I didn't comply by turning tail and leaving them to fight the monsters alone, their eyes held a level of doubt in me that my superior officer had also shown right before he declared me a traitor and sentenced me to death.

Some of these soldiers recognized me from the multiple fights we waged in the past. They knew my reputation, and they stood fast, with their weapons aimed at the hungry beasts, looking every bit as scared as I felt. We were only ten wide, and I had a moment to wonder whether this was all that was left after Mikhail's destruction.

Only two of the soldiers carried super soakers. It would have been better odds if everyone carried the magic juice that disabled leviathans. Bullets wouldn't do a damn thing but irritate them unless we could compromise their defenses. Which meant bleach on their iron skin. It was the only way to make them vulnerable. However, with Mikhail behind us, if we could soak the mothers with bleach, Mikhail's fire could kill them without anyone wasting bullets.

Assuming he isn't a complete murderous dick.

I glanced over my shoulder at Mikhail. The orange in his chest turned red and yellow as he stared downtown. His gaze moved to mine, and he gave me a nod, as if he knew I was expecting him to have my back. I glanced at the growing pool of blood surrounding him and turned back to the ones who had done him harm. If I could, I would torch every single one of them myself.

I need to get hold of my emotions before they give me whiplash.

We only had one shot at this. Even with my misgivings of Mikhail's alliances, I assumed he wouldn't cook the soldiers while I was among them. I shifted under the weight of his duplicity. He never put me in harm's way before, so I had to trust he would keep that pattern now, despite still wanting to thrash him raw for what he did.

Instead of dwelling on whether or not he was on our side, I made sure my spray bottle was on stream. I pointed it at the nearest beast and squeezed the trigger. My stream fell short, but the beast crinkled his nose and stepped farther away. Instead of moving forward, I squeezed again, creating a barrier around us that the beasts stepped back from.

They roared at us but did not rush us like they had done in the past. I wasn't sure whether it was the neat line of bleach or something else.

"Hit them in the face or the chest if you can," I said to the ones with the soakers. I received curt nods as they pumped the guns, ramping up the pressure.

I glanced behind me at Mikhail. Was he the reason the beasts weren't charging? The blaze in his chest had turned blue, and smoke drifted from his nostrils. He wasn't looking at the leviathans like earlier; instead, he looked at the soldier on the right with a super soaker.

I moved in behind the soldier, facing Mikhail while I handed off my bottle of bleach to the soldier next to the one with a super soaker. I switched the gun from my right hand, which had been compromised, and steadied it in my left hand, aiming it right between Mikhail's eyes, shaking my head slowly.

He met my gaze, and his eyes flicked up at the Serpent King and then back at me as if some sick deal had been made between them.

"Go!" I yelled. The bleach ripped out of both soakers, followed by the roar of the leviathan. "So help me God, Mik, I will shoot you if you don't take out the monsters," I growled, low.

His glare told me more than I wanted, but he let his fire loose, sweeping his head above our heads and across the line of monsters. The screams of the leviathans were much louder than the death cries of the baby leviathans in the subway had been. But when they all fell silent, followed by thuds that shook the ground, I chanced a glance down Broadway at the Serpent King.

The Serpent King hissed, and his glare was aimed right at Mikhail, as if he had done something unforgivable this time. I had heard that hiss before. It was his call to arms. Which meant we had very little time to move before we were overrun by monsters. And this time, a small barrier of bleach would not hold back the herd.

"Retreat!" I yelled. The soldiers listened, ducking toward the west end subway entrance. I went to follow and then whirled around, meeting Mikhail's resigned gaze.

"Go." He nodded his head toward the soldiers.

Mikhail would be ripped to shreds if I left him to the beasts.

I aimed my gun at the clasp on the anchor in the ground and shot three times, praying the bullet wouldn't ricochet and harm either one of us, This was my only choice to break the iron hold on Mikhail. He couldn't fly away, not with his wings so destroyed. But he could run with the rest of us.

I grabbed the mangled chain and yanked him toward the subway entrance the rest of the team had ducked into. Mikhail in dragon form would never fit down the stairway and I spun, waving the troops down to safety before I turned to Mikhail. I pointed the gun at him. "Shift," I commanded.

"I can't." He met my gaze.

"You can't fly away either, and you can't fit down in the tunnels in your current form. So, shift, damn it."

"I cannot shift." He held out his shredded wings. "I need to heal first, or I will bleed out."

"Then figure out how to fucking fit down these stairs!" I yanked on the chain, pulling him with me as I hobbled down the steps. I focused on moving as fast as I could because the ground shook as thousands of leviathans raced up the streets of New York. Mikhail had to know death was coming at us at a speed we could not counter. I would pull him down here if it killed me because although I wanted to strangle the man, I could not let the dragon be ripped to pieces on my watch. "If you don't figure out a way to downsize, whether it's shifting, or becoming the incredible shrinking dragon, I will die with you. I can't leave you behind, no matter how much I want to."

The sound of metal clanking on the ground spun me back around. A mini-dragon the size of a wild turkey lay on the top step, caught underneath the large iron collar that had fit his massive form.

I hurried back up the steps and maneuvered the collar so he could get out. The moment he was free from the weight of the iron, I scooped him up under my arm, ignoring the stretch in my back. I limped quickly down the stairs and jumped the turnstiles, sprinting past the waiting soldiers. They followed me down onto the southbound tracks and I turned south, running as fast as I could into the deeper tunnels, flying blind in the near total darkness. The meager flashlights tried to pierce the blackness, but they only lit a few feet in front of us at a time. Tile panels fell from the ceiling as we ran, and the entire floor shook as if an earthquake ripped the ground apart.

When my adrenaline started to fade, my pace slowed until I couldn't take another step. My wrists throbbed and my back and legs felt as if they were on fire. I was sure I had done damage to my healing body again, and that knowledge sapped the strength right out of me. The rest of the soldiers surrounded us, but it was the darkness of the subway passage that pressed down on me until I couldn't take another step.

"I need to rest," I said.

"Will do, Sarge," one of the men said.

Then a dull light swung back in my direction, blinding me.

My eyes slowly adjusted enough to make out the shapes around me. I blinked at the line of soldiers in front of me, all of which had their guns pointed in my direction.

The largest one, with bright, accusing eyes, stared at me. "That thing knew your name." He nodded toward the dragon nestled under my arm.

I nodded and took a breath. How was I even going to explain this without them pulling the trigger? I slowly lowered to the ground and put Mikhail down at my side, protecting him with my arm. "It's a long story and one I do not have the energy to recount right now, so if you are going to shoot us, go ahead. I'm too tired to argue at the moment."

"I saved her," Mikhail said. "She is just returning the favor."

"How did you save her?" the soldier asked.

"She was sent to Grand Central and did not know that the leviathans and Serpent King were not interested in a peace treaty. They want to stomp out the human race, and I do not agree with them." He raised his fractured wings. "As you can see, they did not take too kindly to my traitorous acts."

Mikhail's wings did not look quite as bad as they had on the street. Some of the webbing had reformed, but it was translucent like a baby bat's wing and traversed by bloody scratches. He was still stunning to look at in the low light. His scales rippled with colors every time he moved. It was surreal, staring at him while he was so small.

One kick could send him careening down the tunnel, and I had a moment to relish that vision. Then I shook the image out of my head and took another look at his damaged wings. A slow realization hit, and I had to ask.

"How many times have they shredded those?" I asked, interrupting their interrogation.

He turned his citrine eyes on me. "Once before."

I closed my eyes. It all made sense now. I couldn't understand why he didn't fight back when they killed his family. He physically could not, and dragon fire, like bullets, only served to annoy the beasts when their armor wasn't compromised.

"Why did you destroy the museum and our stash of bleach?" I asked, coming back to the reason I wanted to see him suffer by my hand and no other's.

He looked down at the ground. "I told you. I had coffee before that farce of a court-martial."

The cock of a gun drew my attention back on the soldiers.

"You were court-martialed?"

"I can torch your asses before you pull any one of those triggers, so I suggest you put away the damn guns before I lose my patience." Mikhail's chest started glowing orange.

"Do not threaten them," I snapped. "You violated my trust and killed my platoon and who knows how many others with your caffeine-induced fire path."

Mikhail's wide eyes turned to mine.

"I don't give a flying fuck that you are the last goddamned dragon. You fried all that bleach we brought back from that stock room. Did you even think about that while you were leveling Manhattan?"

Gun barrels slowly dropped to the ground as the firing line in front of us witnessed me tearing the dragon a new one.

Mikhail pointed his wing at me. "I lost control and aimed my fire away from where you were. If I hadn't, you would not be here. And yes, I focused it on the bastards who tried to kill you. They would have tried again had I not taken them out. Unfortunately, the bleach went up in flames, too."

"I could wring your neck," I muttered and unclasped my backpack, setting it down so I could lean on the sturdy fabric. I wiped my face and glanced up at the soldiers. "We were court-martialed for treason." I pointed between me and Mikhail. "And chained to the statue at the entrance of the park."

They looked between us, cocking their heads like confused puppies. Their gazes jumped from the mini-dragon to me.

I held out my wrists so they could see my latest injuries. "Did you know those chains had spikes to keep people from escaping?"

Their eyes widened enough for me to see the whites clearly in the minimal light.

"Yeah. I guess that must have been something new, courtesy of Commander Adams."

"Commander Adams was a dick. I saw him steal the medals he didn't earn off your former commander's uniform." The soldier who seemed the youngest spoke, but from his mannerisms, I guessed he was actually one of the more senior members of this little platoon. Although I had never run into him on the streets. "But I still don't understand how they chained a dragon to the statue with you."

"The dragon is Mikhail St. Clare." I hooked my thumb toward Mikhail.

"Big Mik?" one of the ones shrouded in darkness asked, his voice cracking.

"Yup. Imagine my surprise when he shifted at Grand Central Station." I huffed and sent a sideways glare at the one who had actually saved my life multiple times since that failed negotiation.

"Dragons can shift?" the young leader asked.

"Apparently only Mikhail can shift. So no, not all dragons, only this arrogant asshole here." I waved at my cohort.

Guns cocked again, and I caught the nuance of change from interested to betrayed. I knew that feeling. I wouldn't blame them if they blasted him into next week, but I couldn't let them. I still had that small seed of hope that he would follow through on his promise to rid Manhattan of the terrorists.

"He is our only hope to take down the leviathans. You've seen his path of destruction and he's a tech genius from the old life. So, he knows how to make a bomb made with bleach," I added and then glared at him. "But we need to find more bleach now that he destroyed our stash."

"Do you trust him?" Hard, bright eyes peered over the barrel of a gun.

I glanced at the soldier who asked the million-dollar question and bit my lip. Did I trust Mikhail after what he did? It was not an easy answer, and I was too tired to care.

"I don't know how to answer you. I was marching downtown to find him and skin him alive after what he did to the museum. But seeing as he has not turned *you* to dust yet..." I shrugged. "I don't know his endgame, but I do know he has walked among us long before the monsters came. Hell, long before any of us were even born. So, it's your call." I waved at the guns. "Your choice to possibly save humanity or doom us to extinction."

4

I guess my "done with this shit" attitude impacted the soldiers in a positive way. They backed off and let us be for the moment, shuffling enough of a distance away so their quiet voices didn't carry to my ears. But I was sure Mikhail could hear because his ears twitched quite a bit and he kept his head so that one of his ears faced the group.

"You really thought I did that on purpose?" he asked softly.

My gaze fell on him instead of the shadows down the tunnel. I nodded. "You *are* a dragon."

He sent a cross glare in my direction and then looked away. "Have you learned nothing over the past month?"

I went to make a snide remark, but I closed my mouth. Mikhail had shown me more decency than my own platoon leader, even after he finally pried the secret of the bleach out of me. He could have easily turned me to ash along with everyone else, but he didn't. I glanced at my wrist and could just make out the bandage in the darkness. The bandage Mikhail had put on me before he set the city on fire.

Instead of dealing with the swirl of emotion building inside me, I focused my attention on our little band of soldiers. "Where's the rest of your platoon?" I called loud enough for them to turn toward my voice. If we were going to make it out of this alive, we would need more manpower than ten bodies and an injured dragon. Although, if Mikhail healed up quickly, he was like his own army.

What appeared to be the leader of the group came forward. "This is all that's left, ma'am." He was young and did not act like a militia member. He stood at attention like a true military soldier.

Damn. "I'm sorry." I didn't know what else to say.

"The past few weeks have been bloody." He glanced at Mikhail and then back at me. "They wanted to know where the last dragon was, and they slaughtered civilians and militia alike trying to find your... friend."

I jerked at the term and glanced at Mikhail. "I'm not sure I'd categorize him as my friend." I spoke slowly, trying to work this all out with a mind that was overtired and trying to catch up with everything that occurred since Mikhail whisked me away from Grand Central Station.

The soldier let out a small laugh. "If nothing else, the dragon considers you a friend. Or an ally. He wouldn't have told you to run otherwise."

I noted an underlying tone of disgust and met the soldier's sharp and accusing eyes. "If I *had* run, none of you would be here." I slid my gaze to Mikhail. "Isn't that right, Mikhail?" They needed to know what he almost did at the Serpent King's bidding.

Mikhail's head lowered. If he had been in human form, his cheeks would have burned red with embarrassment. "I agreed to their terms. I agreed to be bait so they could extinguish whatever resistance was still out there. If I died, they didn't care, but if I agreed to torch any humans who crawled out of the tunnels, I would be allowed to live as their..." He swallowed and his throat seemed to constrict. "As their pet," he said softly enough for the air to chill around me. "It was a matter of survival." His eyes lifted to mine. "But if they ever get their hands on me again, there will be no bargaining for my life."

His words caused a red veil to fall over my eyes, and my left fist shot out, smashing into the side of his snout, knocking him over. I shook the sting out of my hand and looked up at the soldier as if I didn't just punch a dragon.

"What's your name?" I asked as he stared with his mouth open in shock.

"Um." He looked between Mikhail struggling to get back on his feet and me. "Troy Harrington," he said. "And you just punched a dragon. You have a death wish or something?"

Mikhail chuckled as he rubbed his jaw with his tattered wing. "I think she does, but she'll never admit it."

I glared at Mikhail and pointed my finger at him. "You don't know a damn thing about me, so don't profess to know me just because you took care of me for a month."

His eyes narrowed. "Don't test me, human," he growled.

"Fuck you, dragon," I snarled back at him, ready to strike him down again.

Troy slowly backed up a few steps facing his palms toward the two of us. "I'm not sure either of you are safe to be around. I think I'll just take my men somewhere..."

"There *is* nowhere to go," Mikhail snapped. "The minute you show yourselves on the streets, they'll slaughter you. She is your best bet on surviving. And as much as it pains me, she is mine as well."

I huffed and turned my shoulder away from Mikhail, meeting Troy's sharp gaze. "You asked me if I trusted him?" I shook my head slowly. "No. But here's the shit thing. He has the brains and the fire capacity, along with a hell of a strong motive to destroy the leviathans and the Serpent King. And that is what I'm betting on here. Not his loyalty to the human race, which is fleeting at best, but his desire to strike the monsters down himself."

Troy pursed his lips as he digested my words. "I still think you two are a breeze away from an explosion." He crossed his arms. "But I will follow you since the dragon also thinks you are the one who will be our savior. However, if I think either of you are putting my men in danger, I will not hesitate to take you out."

I would have done the same for my team had they still been alive. I gave Troy a nod and then leaned against the backpack as exhaustion took over. "You might want those bleach barrels aimed in both directions. The leviathans have sent their young into the tunnels before," I said through a yawn, and then lay my head down, leaving my welfare in the hands of these strangers.

5

The sound of hissing cries filled the space, jerking me from sleep. The brightness in the tunnel made me momentarily wonder whether the leviathans punched through the pavement above us. But the stench that followed made that idea die as surely as the baby leviathans succumbed to Mikhail's fire.

Gunfire erupted in the opposite direction and Mikhail spun and ran weaving through the legs of the soldiers to the front of the line before spewing out another blast of fire that decimated the new attackers. Baby leviathans screamed, and I covered my ears.

When the noise faded, silence followed, and the team gathered closer around me. Once

Mikhail breached the tiny circle, I stared at him. His wings were more solid now and he looked steadier on his feet than he had when I fell asleep.

"We need to get them to a safe space," I said, unsure he would agree to have a small delegation of strangers in his home base.

He nodded and looked south. He glanced at the soaker guns and the half empty spray bottle. "We need more bleach. Otherwise, we won't make it. I can guarantee they are feeding their young into the subway systems downtown, so the closer we get, the more we will encounter."

Hitting up another custodial closet at Grand Central was no longer an option, but that wasn't the only hub in Manhattan. "Are there custodial closets at Penn Station?"

His eyebrows rose, as if I had surprised him. "Probably. But wouldn't you have hit those places already?"

I know our platoon never thought of hitting up custodial closets in the subway stations. Schools, yes, but subway stations, not so much. We didn't even try hotels, either. I glanced at the soldiers. "Have you?"

They shook their heads. "We didn't even consider subway stations for having bleach." Troy's eyes lit up at the prospect. "Schools and hospitals we emptied out as soon as we found out about the leviathans' weakness."

They were just as shortsighted as we were. "Did anyone bother to search hotels?" Heads shook. There were plenty of those around. "Or the convention center?" Again, heads shook. So, we now had some other locations to search for our new form of ammunition along the way to Mikhail's.

I glanced at Mikhail. Having him on his feet in the front of the pack would be beneficial, but seeing as we were attacked from both sides, we needed more bleach delivery options. Otherwise, we would run out of firepower pretty quickly. We needed more hands to carry stuff, too, if we happened on another stash like we found at Grand Central.

"I think we are going to need you in human form. Can you shift yet?" I asked him, eyeing his mended wings.

He stretched them out and glanced at the whisper-thin membranes and red lines still traversing the material. "Not quite there yet," he said. "I'd be a hindrance to the team in human form right now." He met my gaze. "Another day and I should be good."

"In another day, we'll be knee-deep in leviathan babies," I snapped. I didn't have the patience for his healing that he had had with mine. The longer he remained as this tiny dragon, the more danger we were in, and I certainly wasn't in fighting shape. I just wanted to get to a place of safety before we encountered something unsurmountable. I narrowed my eyes and pointed at him. "Are you trying to sabotage our efforts?"

"He gave us a heads-up before the leviathans arrived." Troy waved at the cooked messes on both sides of us. "He didn't have to do that," he added.

Troy sticking up for Mikhail did not help my mood.

"We wouldn't be in this predicament had the damn dragon not destroyed our stash of bleach," I grumbled at them and turned away, checking my emotions. I took the time to dissect my response to make sure I wasn't reacting with feelings alone. I could not wrap my head around a vulnerable Mikhail. I mean, when he had been knocked out in the garage, when he came to, he took control again. Even as an injured mini-dragon, he was still a force to be reckoned with. But I didn't know how fast he could move, and if he held us up, that would only make it easier for the leviathans to multiply and send their offspring to their death in the hopes that we would run out of fuel or firepower in the process.

And looking at our reserves, that was a very high possibility. It was like being buried alive and watching as the last of the oxygen bled out, snuffing out the last match and plunging your last struggling breaths into darkness and despair.

I shivered at the thought and refocused. Although I would push myself for the cause, I did not think Mikhail would do the same. Not if it did not suit his end goal. He only had one focus in mind, and if we jeopardized it, he would sacrifice us to get his revenge.

The one thing we had in our favor: like us, Mikhail was now a prime target for extinction.

6

Mikhail and I took the front of the pack with Troy on one side of me and Jenny with her super soaker on the other side of Mikhail. Karl, the other super-soaker soldier, took up the back along with Adam, who manned the spray bottle. The rest of the soldiers were sandwiched in between us.

We followed the Seventh Avenue express tracks south from Times Square. I hadn't run as far as I thought I did when we escaped the monsters. I hadn't even come close to the eight blocks to reach Penn Station. We made our way past the signage for the station, which seemed like it was only a few city blocks from where we left the dead leviathans.

"Stay put. Let me scope out the station to see if I can locate the custodial closets and anything we can pirate to carry bulk loads of bleach with," Mikhail said.

"Bullshit," I spat back. I wasn't about to trust him on his own.

"Excuse me?" He gawked at me, and so did a few of the soldiers.

"You are not stepping out of my sight. And if I catch you signaling to your monster friends out on the street, I'll put a bullet in your brain." I narrowed my eyes in a glare. "And where you go, we all follow. I'm not leaving these soldiers down here in the dark to be massacred by baby leviathans."

That earned me a cocked eyebrow from Troy. "We can handle..."

I turned on him, pointing my finger like a teacher who caught her student cheating on a test. "Nope. I'm not sacrificing anyone. Understand?"

"No disrespect, but that is not your call." Troy crossed his arms. "These are my soldiers, my responsibility. It's our war, too."

I gave him the once over. "How long have you been leading troops?"

His lips twitched into a smile. "Ten years. You?"

He was out of his mind. There was no way he led troops for ten years. We hadn't even been at war that long. "No fucking way. Not unless you started while you were still in grade school." My response earned me some snickers from his group.

"Sweetheart, I'm almost forty. I went into the Marine Corps the day I turned eighteen and worked my way onto the Delta Force."

I stared at him, and he smirked, causing me to realize my mouth had dropped open at the declaration of his age. I wouldn't have put him at even close to thirty. He looked damn good for his age. I popped my lips together, trying not to blush, but the heat in my cheeks told me I failed.

He continued, "When the world turned to shit, my mother fell ill, so I was on leave here in the city. Everyone else in Delta Force had been on base when the dragons came, but I wasn't there." His lips pressed tightly together. "I am the only Delta Force member left." He glared at Mikhail as if it were his fault, which was likely the case, because he commanded the dragon forces before they were slaughtered by the Serpent King. "Instead of joining one of the other militias that were being formed, I took a different route. I had no interest in businessmen and women thinking they knew tactical warfare better than I did, so I built this team from the inner-city gangs. They had the knowledge, skills, and raw nerve that I needed, and they were all itching to get back at these things that had stolen their livelihood."

I glanced around at the men and woman following him. They were a mix of all races, Blacks, Asians, Hispanics, and Whites, and there was only one other woman in the mix. But they all had one thing in common: that hard edge I remembered from the street kids I had run into on the subways. I used to try to avoid being in the same subway car as gang members because the likelihood of a White Upper West Side girl walking out unscathed was higher than being left alone by gang members.

"These are the best and the brightest in the city. I didn't just take anyone from the gang pool. They had to meet *my* standards and pass my boot camp to make the team. And everyone who made the cut had to bring their gang's armory to the table. All that firepower is what sustained us. Gangs were the only entities that still had semi-automatic weapons and an arsenal of bullets that would make the military proud."

I blinked and looked closer at the weapons they held. They weren't the normal rifles or handguns I was accustomed to. The fact they carried that kind of firepower actually gave me more hope that we'd make it to Mikhail's—as long as they still had ammunition.

He glanced around at what was left of his team. Pride filled his eyes and made his chest puff out. When his gaze returned to mine, it was icy with resolve. "These soldiers are my only surviving family. You have no place in making decisions for us."

Well, shit. How could I argue with him now?

"I don't care what your credentials are. The only one *I* take orders from is Holly," Mikhail said, cutting through whatever standoff might occur. "And without the dragon on your side, you have no hope of winning this war."

"Shut up," I snapped at Mikhail. I didn't need him throwing his testosterone into the pot. It was already boiling over with Troy. And although Troy's former Delta Force status impressed me, I still didn't like being the one subservient to a leader when I had no knowledge of track records beyond what he just spewed out.

"And how many have died because of shoddy leadership?" I asked.

"None of my trained soldiers have died. I can't say the same for those who were sent by other platoons to help round out my team, though." This time his smile turned almost feral. "They didn't particularly like my style of leadership."

I stepped closer, puffing my chest as if I were taller than this Delta Force guy, but I could only get within a head's height of him. Looking up into his hard eyes, I knew I failed at my intimidation tactic. At this very moment, Troy reminded me of the way Mikhail was when we had first been at his apartment in lower Manhattan. All business, with the force behind him.

Troy glared down at me as if I were just an annoying gnat.

"Troy, stop being a dick." Jenny brushed a piece of her dark hair out of her face. She slipped a piece of peppermint gum between her teeth. "I heard she got fried by a dragon and lived. She's not one of those prissy little girls from Brooklyn who cries if her nail breaks."

I didn't break my stare, but I appreciated what the little Hispanic girl said. She was compact and muscular, like that chick in those old fast car movies. I bet she was just as fierce. Especially considering Troy's left eye twitched just enough for me to catch his displeasure about being questioned in a public forum.

"Is she right?" he asked.

"Yes, I did get burned by a dragon, but it wasn't from running away." Because my platoon and nearly all the others fighting for our survival had been decimated, I owed it to these soldiers to come clean. "I wasn't exactly forthcoming with my superior officers, because they had no idea that Mikhail was a dragon." I stepped back out of Troy's personal space. "For some reason, Mikhail put his trust in me and got me out of Grand Central under false pretenses." I glanced at the mini-dragon. "He wanted to know our secret. How we were actually taking down the leviathans."

"And you told him?" Troy crossed his arms.

"Oh hell no. Not at first. I wanted to get back to my platoon, but he wouldn't allow it. He said it was too dangerous and since a body was dropped with a note declaring that I had screwed up the negotiations, he didn't think I'd be welcomed without some serious fabricating of stories." I glanced at Mikhail.

"So, the dragon offered to burn you." Troy sneered at Mikhail.

"No. That was my plan."

Troy's gaze snapped to mine. "Excuse me?"

"It seemed logical at the time, but on retrospect, my commander was going to sacrifice me to the monsters no matter what story I concocted. I could have walked in the door with the dragon on a leash and he still would have court-martialed me." I shrugged and turned, pulling up the hem of my shirt so they all could see my back.

"I advised against her plan," Mikhail piped in from enough of a distance away to avoid a swat or a kick from me.

"So, you lied to your commander," Troy said.

I turned and nodded. "Yes. They would have shot him on sight had he been in dragon form, and still put me out for the monsters to tear to pieces. But Mikhail has the technology to make that bleach bomb. He can decimate their army and give us half a chance. I put my money on him for our survival." I glared sideways at the fiend. "And I still am, despite my misgivings."

Troy's sharp gaze fell on the dragon. "How did you care for wounds that grave?" He waved at me.

"I have the means and materials. I was married to a human woman who raised my children," he said, as if that made any difference. "Accidents happened."

"You have a wife and kids?" Jenny asked.

Mikhail slowly shook his head. "They made me watch as they tore them limb from limb." His chest glowed as his voice turned feral. "That was after they decimated the rest of the dragons."

"They killed a dragon after the last body drop," Troy said.

"Yes. Ricky, the only one who truly believed in their cause to wipe out the stain of humanity from the earth."

"And why did they not kill you?" Karl stepped into the field of light.

"Because I was still useful. I'm the only one who could shift, and they wanted me to infiltrate your ranks, locate your platoons, and destroy them."

"Well, you certainly did that with your path of fire," I interjected, wondering whether he was still following the monsters' orders in some way.

"That was not my intention," Mikhail snapped at me. "I had coffee because I could feel the animosity in that place. Your life was as good as over the minute we stepped in that building. I thought they'd put us in front of a firing line, not out on the street as bait for leviathans." His wings fluttered with the snarl coming from his snout. "I had a coffee, knowing that I would need enough fire power to melt bullets before they got to you. So, fucking sue me." He sauntered off in the direction of the platform to Penn Station.

Troy traded a glance with Jenny, and she smirked.

"Seems the dragon is a bit smitten with you," she said, sounding quite the opposite of a gang kid.

Maybe Troy was the type of leader who could drive the gang mentality right out of kids and replace it with a fierce loyalty that my troops seemed to have for me. Even so, her statement was off the mark by miles.

"The fuck you say?" I cocked an eyebrow at her.

This time Troy let out a laugh. "You really don't see it." He hooked his thumb toward the dragon.

"Mikhail tolerates me," I said. "That's the extent of it." I glanced after the stomping mini-dragon. He looked like a child who had just been told to go to his room. But he was headed in the direction we told him he couldn't go alone. I started after him, followed by the rest of the snickering soldiers.

I spun around and pointed at them collectively. "Stop that," I hissed and then turned to continue after my dragon, wondering whether they were right and just how I would take that after everything we had been through. His actions in the garage came to the forefront of my mind. He hadn't even looked at me that night with anything remotely like attraction or affection.

That little voice in the back of my mind piped up. *Yes, but he had just retrieved the heads of his family from Grand Central. You wouldn't be frisky either if the tables were turned.*

It always burned at the pit of my stomach when that voice was right.

# 7

Mikhail led us up to the ground floor of the station and signaled for us to stay low and stay quiet. I pointed back to the underground floor we just traversed. And he shook his head.

"No storage rooms," he whispered.

The one we found at Grand Central was on the platform level, but Penn Station didn't seem to have any gradually rising platforms into the heart of the station like Grand Central had on the main lines. Here it was all stairs or narrow pathways. Understanding clicked, but I still didn't like the exposure. Some of the glass ceiling panels had already been destroyed and each step we took ground crushed glass under our feet.

He led us in the direction of one of the bigger department stores, and when we got to the metal gate, he waved us back with his wing. Mikhail crawled up the gate until his front paws were high enough to match the tallest soldier and he spread his paws three feet wide. His lower legs stretched out in the same pattern but only reached about halfway down the gate. It didn't take long for the metal to turn red between his four paws. He yanked backward and fell onto his back in front of us.

"What the—" Troy said.

"Shush." Mikhail cut him off and then rolled to his side and gently placed the grid on the ground. He repeated with the lower half and then walked through the opening as quietly as possible.

We all followed.

He pointed to the row of neatly stacked carts with the store's logo on it as we passed. A couple of soldiers grabbed carts and followed. Thankfully, they didn't grab any with squeaky wheels. That would have doomed us. When we passed the household cleaner section, Mikhail raised a wing and halted. The soldiers with the carts marched down the aisle and picked up the few bleach bottles still nestled on the shelf.

Mikhail then led us to the back where a locked door stood between us and the back office and storage area of the store. When he raised up to put his paws on the locking mechanism, I cleared my throat.

"Look, if there's a stash back there that's bigger than what we found at Grand Central, I don't want to fry the only lock that will keep it safe. Give me a second." I put up a finger. I went to the cooking utensil section and found some slim fondue pokers. When I returned, I received quite a few raised eyebrows. "I wasn't exactly an angel in my youth," I whispered.

My misspent youth had involved some level of breaking and entering. Thus, my skills at opening locks. Just because my family had come from Uptown, didn't mean I didn't dance along the line of the law. Thankfully, this wasn't one with a keypad. Otherwise, I would have let Mikhail melt the door because a keypad needs electricity to work. The light from the glass front of the store didn't reach this far back and I had to have Jenny point her flashlight at the hole. With three kebab sticks in place, I turned the set to the left as one unit.

I was rewarded with a click and then I reached down and pulled on the door handle. The door swished open, and I smiled, waving the soldiers inside. I glanced down at Mikhail, waving him along, too.

The door swung closed behind me, silently drenching us in darkness. The flashlight Jenny had didn't penetrate much. All I could see were shadows of shelving. The rest of the flashlights came to life, illuminating aisles and aisles of packed shelving, as if the store got a new shipment right before all hell broke loose in Manhattan. Fortunately for us, the store didn't have frozen foods. Otherwise, this place would stink of rot enough to make me want to barf.

We had raided some of the closed grocery stores once or twice in the beginning and those places were gag-worthy. It took at least a week to get that stench out of our clothes and it seemed to linger in our nostrils for much longer.

Still, the sight of fully stocked shelves stopped us all in our tracks. This place had not been raided, and I wondered what kind of locks they had to the outside world beyond the iron gate at the entrance that was immovable when locked tight. I had had some experience trying to break into those things. Most were locked forever without electricity to run the keypads controlling them.

The door protecting this little gold mine wasn't one that could be knocked in, either. So, with Mikhail's help, we had hit the motherload—as long as the rats hadn't gotten in here first. The only sound was of the two carts rolling on the floor as we slowly walked through the warehouse. All I could think was the carts we had would not be big enough. If I had my way, I'd bring the industrial-size cases of cereal and chips with us, but I knew better, especially considering Mikhail just kept walking and scanning the aisles. His nails clacked on the concrete floor, mixing with the rolling wheels, and it seemed like a lot more noise than it had through the store. Perhaps it was the darkness bearing down on all of us from all sides of this storeroom.

He stopped and flicked his wing down one of the rows ahead. I'd say he was grinning, but the shadows were too unpredictable. When I rounded the corner and flashlights hit the shelving, I inhaled sharply.

I thought the stash in the supply closet at Grand Central was big, but this dwarfed that stash by a multiplier of seven or eight times the number of bleach bottles.

"We might need a few more carts," he said softly, with eyes that were possibly wider than mine.

"Spread out," Troy whispered. "See what we can find in here to transport this stuff with minimal noise." The soldiers dispersed and returned a few minutes later with laundry carts, yard carts, and wheelbarrows.

We filled every container, including the shopping carts, until we could pack no more in without fear of containers falling during our trek back through Penn Station. We had five containers and some of them would require multiple trips up and down the staircases to the lower levels due to the sheer volume and weight, but it would be worth it if we could get all these packages to Mikhail's apartment building.

"Grab as many backpacks as they have and pack them with whatever food fits. We can double up packs, if need be, but we can't pass up on this opportunity," Troy ordered. "And if they have any super soakers in the toy section, grab those and we can fill up with what's still on the shelves before we go."

I traded a glance with Mikhail and then went to grab some of the cereal boxes I saw. Milk or no milk, having my pick of cereals was like stepping into heaven. I was still amazed this place hadn't been picked over at all, but I was beyond thankful for the stock that was still here.

Once everyone gathered at the storage room door, we each took an extra backpack filled with food, and ripped into the super soaker packages. There were enough for every soldier to have at least one mega soaker and one smaller one. We filled every one of the toy weapons with bleach, getting ready for the perilous trek back to the subway floor.

"Be alert," Troy said as we filtered out of the storage room as quietly as we could with our overloaded packs and carts.

I paused at the door and finagled the skewers in the lock, clicking it back into place before I pocketed my new lockpick fondue set. I wanted to make sure what was in this storeroom was kept secure in case we needed to make the trip back for any reason.

I received a nod from both Troy and Mikhail as if they had the same thing on their mind.

We made our way through the store to the opening in the security gate and filtered through. Even at our quietest, the carts still crunched the glass under the wheels loud enough for me to shiver. In the tunnels, it would be louder which meant the baby leviathans would find us quicker.

I recited a silent prayer for God to thank him for letting us find such a stash and asked for the Holy Spirit to be with us on this trek, because we needed a miracle for all of us to get to our destination alive.

8

Mikhail led us to an internal ramp that traversed back and forth down to the lower level, where we should be safer. I never knew this wheelchair ramp existed. I just thought the handicapped people took the elevators, but this suited our purpose better than the labor-intensive climb down the stairs would have been considering the elevators were all defunct without power.

He led us to the southern-most ramp to the Seventh Avenue express line and then put his wings up, halting all of us. "Soak the ramp," he hissed.

We rapidly pumped our guns and let loose on the darkness below. The screams of burning monsters filled the space, followed by a plume of fire that lit up the tracks below, along with at least a dozen baby leviathans.

We marched forward, with our soakers aimed into the tunnel, but there seemed to be no more. Soldiers took turns covering while we got all the carts down onto the tracks. With our stash secured between us, we started a full jog, pushing carts of bleach along with us.

"Hold up," Mikhail said as he stopped.

"What is it?" I tried to make out anything in the dark in front of me. I heard an inhale and passed the procured flashlight over the area in front of us. The light passed over the hunched dragon. He was bigger than the little turkey-sized beast he had been since we fled Times Square. His eyes flashed in my direction in warning. I turned the flashlight farther down the tunnel while pumping my super soaker. The rest of the soldiers followed suit. The hiss of pressure building in the toys filled the small space but none of us saw what had made Mikhail stop.

Bleach dripped on my hands. The sharp stench drifted to my nose. We were all ready to take out monsters, but none came. "Mik?" I whispered.

"Just another minute," he said with a voice so strained that my flashlight moved to where he had been.

All I saw were human legs. Bare human legs. I stared. The last time I saw him shift from dragon to human, he was clothed, not naked and sweaty like he was now. His eyes flashed at me.

"Do you mind," he growled with teeth that were still dragon-like. Fabric still webbed between his arms and his torso.

I turned away and stared at Troy's shocked expression.

"This wasn't what it was like when he shifted before," I said. "At Grand Central, his shift was instantaneous. One moment, he was a dragon; the next, he was human. And he had clothes on."

Troy turned his gaze to me, cocking an eyebrow at me as if he didn't believe me.

"It's a little harder to shift when I'm injured." Mikhail's voice carried in the dark. "I threw a pair of jogging pants and a shirt on the top of one of the bins. Can someone bring that to me?"

Shuffling and then one of the soldiers shoved the clothes at me as if he were afraid of approaching the dragon now that he was in human form. Of course, the mini-dragon wasn't as intimidating as Mikhail St. Clare in human form. He was a monster of a man. Over six five and built like a Mack truck.

I stepped forward with the light pointed at the ground and reached the clothing out to him. I guess he expected one of the men to bring him clothing, not me.

Even so, he took them and slowly put the shirt over his head with a wince. He got one leg in the pants and then glanced at me. "Turn."

I did, and then his hand landed on my shoulder. But it wasn't steady as he balanced on one leg to fit his other into the free pant leg. His warmth penetrated my body like a welcoming embrace. Having his hand on me unearthed the feelings I had buried under my anger at his fiery actions.

"Why did you shift?" I whispered over my shoulder, trying to sweep these unwanted desires away like last month's trash.

"We need to move faster. I was slowing us down."

I hadn't noticed, but then again, I was still in marginal shape after all I was healing from, and the run had been sucking the energy from me. I couldn't imagine going faster. When his hand came off my shoulder, I turned and raised the light to his face. His rugged features were paler than I remembered and although his eyes blazed in an inferno of indignation, I could see the apology written deep in his irises.

"You good now?" I asked without dwelling on his sickly features.

"I am if you are." He glanced at my wrists. "Have you had a chance to redress those?"

"No. And I'm not going to get the chance until we are in your building." I did not want to waste time caring for any of my wounds. If I sat, it would be awhile before I got up again. It looked as though Mikhail might be in the same condition.

"Is there an extra super soaker that I could use?"

I glanced at Troy and received a nod. Someone in the back handed off one to Troy, and he in turn passed it to Mikhail. Although his jaw was tighter than usual and his gaze blazed as he looked at Mikhail. The soldier's dislike of Mikhail now that he had donned his human form was palpable in the air.

"How many of our secrets did you pass to the rest of the monsters?" he asked with a voice that carried a very sharp edge.

Mikhail looked at the child's toy in his hands. "One. The location of her platoon. But only after I destroyed it, and they captured me." He met Troy's gaze. "The rest were always off the mark enough so that the core bases were not harmed."

Troy's gaze narrowed. "But you did participate in killing humans, correct?"

Mikhail nodded. "But you already knew we were responsible for wiping out the military response worldwide." At least he didn't say it with a smile.

It almost sounded as if there were a trace of regret in his words and it took me by surprise.

Troy's hands curled into fists.

"She is the only one who can get away with throwing a punch at me," Mikhail warned and nodded toward me.

Jenny stepped forward. "So, if I decided to kick your ass?" Her voice carried the anger radiating from Troy.

"You would not live to explain your level of stupidity." Mikhail's hard tone was accompanied by a thin trail of smoke drifting from his nostrils.

Jenny's eyebrows drew together as she looked at me and then back at Mikhail. "Why does she get a pass?"

"Because she nearly burned alive and bled for your cause. She earned my respect." His voice was quiet, but his eyes had transformed into that inferno that I now recognized. He was on edge and that meant unpredictability from the dragon.

If he torched the soldiers, he'd torch the bleach. I needed to step in, otherwise, I would shoot him and right now, my heart contracted at the thought.

"When all this is over and we've won this fight, I'll make sure you each get your swipe at him," I said, which earned me a cocked eyebrow from everyone, including Mikhail. "Seriously, if they still are angry enough to throw a punch when this is over, Mikhail is going to *let* each of you punch him." I pointed my finger at Mikhail. "I'll likely be in that line, too."

"I never agreed to that." He turned back to the nearest cart and started away from us. "But *we* don't have time to argue about it. It's time to haul ass."

Mikhail hadn't been kidding, but at least he was jogging at the same pace as the rest of the soldiers. I started out just behind him with Troy on one side and Jenny on the other, but soon I found the pacing a little too much. I fell back into the center of the pack as my body screamed at the exertion.

The pace slowed to a crawl and then stopped. I went to move forward but one of the soldiers put his arm out, stopping me.

"Side. Now!" Mikhail's voice hissed from the front and the scraping of the carts followed as I was pushed to the side wall.

The soldiers hoisted the carts up on the walking path on the side, as we all hugged the wall. The distinct sound of guns pumping filled the darkness and with my back to the concrete tiled wall, the tremors reached into my bones.

"Spray yourselves and the ground in front of us," Mikhail said. "And then remain quiet and very still."

I did as he said, getting my pants and boots wet before creating a line on the floor in front of me. My nose burned from the burst of bleach in the space and my eyes watered. I didn't dare wipe them as I was sure some liquid dripped onto my hands and bleach in the eye was dangerous and painful as hell.

The vibrations in the walls increased until the very ground we stood on felt as if it were going to give at any moment. Even the carts rattled enough for me to shift. A few of the ceiling tiles fell as the stampede got closer. My heart beat as hard and as fast as the vibrations in the wall behind me.

I expected a stampede of baby leviathans. What I didn't expect was light to burst through the ceiling of the tunnel, followed by a grown leviathan's foot. If we had been on the tracks, at least half of us would have been squashed. Another foot slammed through the tunnel a few yards north. The fact the beasts could break through to the tunnels wasn't something that happened often. A few of the shallower passes had been breached this way, but none of the main lines that were deeper set under the surface.

No wonder the world shook violently. The beasts were probably jumping to get the right amount of force to break through. The roadways above would be a god-awful mess and nearly impossible to navigate with the craters this had to be causing to roads without paths underneath. Another foot broke through, near enough to make me shudder.

I glanced at Mikhail, and he slowly shook his head and waved me back against the wall. The rest of the soldiers stood with wide eyes, staring at the destruction of the tunnels. We had a small edge that we were perched on. For some reason, that seemed to be enough to keep us and our treasure out of the destruction zone. If these tunnels had live trains, we would be in dire straits. The subway clearance to the walls was bare inches, and unless you stood in one of the alcoves, you were as dead as if you jumped in front of a moving train.

But it was wide enough for two of the four wheels of each cart to perch on. For the long haul, it would be difficult to balance and move at any fast pace and dropping them onto the tracks would mean that cart was a lost cause, which meant we'd have to carry the heavy containers full of bleach. And if I had read one of the posts right, we still had a distance to travel ahead of us and then we had to cross from the west side to the east side near Brooklyn Bridge. Hell, we hadn't even reached Canal Street.

How much of the subway system had been breached by the leviathans? And were there some areas that were now impenetrable?

My heart dropped, and I glanced back at Mikhail. The deep crevasse between his eyes showed his concentration. The beasts were moving north, not south, but that didn't mean we wouldn't have an ambush down the line.

We needed to find a path that branched out under the buildings and not the streets. All I could think about was the line that went under the site that once held the World Trade Center. It ran under buildings, not streets. At least a portion of it did. There was no way to get there from here without going down the Seventh Avenue express that we were on.

When the wall vibrations lowered, Mikhail cleared his throat, capturing our attention. He picked up his cart, making the muscles in his arms bulge. He nodded toward the rest of the heavy wagons. The soldiers on either side of the containers hoisted theirs and sweat popped out on their brows despite the cool air filtering down into our limited space.

With a silent side shuffle of feet, we moved down the thin path that somehow had saved us from destruction.

"How far?" Troy whispered with a voice full of strain.

"Eighteen blocks and two avenues. Assuming there isn't a section of the tunnel that isn't totally destroyed," Mikhail said in a low hush.

"Fuck."

That was the unanimous response, hissed between strained lips. Those of us not holding a side of a cart had a super soaker at the ready as we shimmied sideways a step at a time, waiting for the next foot to come through the ceiling.

10

$O\!ur$ progress was slow, but we made it to the interchange that would lead us more toward City Hall and the east side rather than continue down the Seventh Avenue path, which had been trashed by the leviathans because it ran directly under the street. Luckily, when we reached the split, it was passable to get from one side of the tracks to the other.

The only problem with the City Hall track: it was a dead end. There was no exit except into City Hall itself. But from the looks of the group, Mikhail included, we all could use a break, and this seemed like a more secure place to get some rest. One way in, and one way out. We just had to be sure to position ourselves under the remains of City Hall and not under the park, where it would be easy for the monsters to crush the tunnel—and us with it.

We still carried the carts, opting for as stealthy an approach as we could. After we got into the safety of the City Hall line, Mikhail stopped and took a bottle of bleach. He drew a line from one side of the entrance to the other, emptying the entire bottle in the process. He set the bottle down at the far side and trotted back to us.

I opened my mouth, and he shook his head, putting his finger on his lips. He pointed topside and twirled his finger. They were close enough for him to sense them. He picked up his cart and continued on until we reached the old entrance to City Hall itself. The small ramp went up into the darkness, but Mikhail led us to the far corner to a door.

He gave a quick glance at the patch of ceiling that let some colored light in and then pointed to me and then to the lock. Just the look to the stained glass above had everyone on edge.

I slid to the door and squinted at the lock as I rummaged in my pocket for the kebabs that I took from the store in Penn Station. This wasn't as easy as the single deadbolt. This had both the handle lock, which was the easy one, but the other lock was much more difficult, especially without a light shining on the lock. But after four tries, I was rewarded with a click.

Mikhail opened the door and waved us all inside the room. Our bodies and carts barely made it, and when Mikhail closed the door, I heard him let out an exhale like we had passed through the bowels of hell and made it out alive. A small light illuminated his hand and he turned, giving us our first look at our current resting space.

It wasn't much. Just a ten-by-ten empty storage room. But with the carts, it left very little room for anyone to move, much less sit down.

"Push the carts against the far wall," Mikhail said softly. "I'll see what I can do to stack them so we can at least take turns getting some rest."

"We've had worse accommodations," Troy said, but he did as Mikhail asked and maneuvered the five carts to the far wall and a couple of folks turned on their flashlights.

With everything stored in one corner, we had a little more room, but Mikhail lifted a couple of the smaller carts onto the larger ones, balancing them so they leaned against the wall. They made sure the wheels were locked on the lower carriages and now we all had the room to find a seat on the ground.

He glanced at me and pointed at my hands. "We need to redress those wounds." He crossed to me. "Did you happen to pack any of those wipes and bandages from your apartment?" He met my gaze.

All eyes were on us standing in the center of the room. I shifted under their stares and nodded as I unclipped my backpack. Now that we weren't moving, every muscle in my body cried out in protest. Everything hurt as I removed the backpacks I carried, and I lowered to a sitting position, handing him the backpack from my apartment. I was too tired to dig through it for the materials he wanted.

I glanced at his wrist as he reached across me. It was healed of the damage the iron spikes had done. Unlike mine. Now that he was focusing on my wrists, the pain flared, reminding me that I was not at my best.

The flame dancing on his fingertips doused as he reached into my pack. A half dozen more flashlights came to life, illuminating the enclosed room.

"Thanks." He pulled out the wipes and liquid bandage tube, along with Band-Aids. He looked at my left wrist first, wiping off the dirt and grime that had built up on my run. He inspected the wound and reapplied the liquid bandage on both sides before covering the hole with crisscrossed Band-Aids. At least the wipes weren't bloody like the last time.

I needed to take off my leather jacket for him to unwrap the bandage that stabilized my right wrist. As he peeled away the wrap, the layers went from damp to reddened on the inside of my wrist. He grimaced and focused on the back of my wrist first. That seemed to be doing as well as my left hand, which I was thankful for.

When he turned my wrist over, I winced at the motion. The blood drained from my face, leaving my skin cold. The room started to spin. He pressed a cool wipe onto my wrist, holding it tight in the same manner he had in my apartment.

"Breathe, Woods," he said, sternly enough to allow me to shake off the sudden wooziness.

I met his gaze, and my chin quivered. "You're not going to cauterize it again, are you?" God, how I hated that pathetic lilt to my voice and the fear that gripped my throat.

He shook his head. "No, you're not hemorrhaging like you were when I first took the shackles out. But I do need to clean the area in order to get another layer of liquid bandage on." He released the pressure on my wrist and started cleaning out the dirt that had found its way between the folds of the Ace bandage.

Relief washed over me, and I swallowed a thin line of bile that had crawled up the back of my throat. I didn't know whether I would remain conscious if he had to cauterize it again. I still don't know how I remained awake and aware last time. Although, his gentle wipes across the puncture wound sent pain spiraling through my bones.

He smiled and shook his head as he continued to clean my wound. "You pointed that gun at me like this hand wasn't as bad off as it is."

"And successfully picked two locks." I forced a smile.

Once he seemed satisfied that the dirt was gone, he put liquid bandage over the wound and let it set before putting on another pair of crisscrossed Band-Aides. He rummaged around in the backpack again and then sighed.

He glanced at me. "You didn't bring the other Ace bandages?"

"No. I had to make a choice, and chocolates won out." I met his gaze and narrowed my eyes at him. If he had been with me when I left my apartment, we would have all the medical supplies he needed to patch me up and then some. He got the message and went back to staring at my broken wrist.

"You have chocolates?" Jenny asked, perking up from her nap.

I reached beyond Mikhail and pulled out the chocolates, tore open the cellophane with my teeth, and opened the box, picking one of my favorites before I handed it to Jenny. There was enough for everyone to have a piece, with a few to spare.

Mikhail added an extra Band-Aid to each side of my wrist and then rebandaged my hand with the soiled wrap so I could function with my right hand as much as I could with my left. Then he straightened one leg and wrapped his arms around his knee, leaning his head down on his elbow.

"You okay?" I asked. His body language screamed exhaustion as much as my muscles did.

He nodded but didn't lift his head. "Sleep." He patted his thigh with his free hand. "You, too."

One by one, the lights turned off, drenching us in darkness. Teeth chattered in the dark as the chill penetrated the room despite the body heat. I wouldn't be surprised if it was snowing on the surface with the arctic blast that seemed to seep through underneath the door.

I would have preferred leaning back-to-back with Mikhail, but he reached out and guided my head down onto his leg. It wasn't as hard as I expected. His muscles were defined but it wasn't like lying on a rock. It was more like lying on a stiff pillow. And he radiated enough heat to take the chill out of the air, but not enough for me to get overheated.

Mikhail's fingers ran through the hair at my temple. The slow drag of it lulled me into a stupor.

Amid the soft snores, I heard the softest of sighs.

"I'm sorry I hurt you," Mikhail whispered and continued his light combing of my hair.

I turned, looking up at where I thought his face would be, and the soft glow of his citrine eyes met mine. I wanted to forgive him but that little voice that has kept me alive all these years wouldn't let me. Not until we were all safe and he was working on that bomb.

"Don't do it again." I turned back and adjusted to get comfortable.

He continued to run his fingers through my hair until his hand came to rest on his thigh and the glow went out. His soft snore added to the sounds filling the room, and I allowed myself to drift off into a restless sleep.

11

I woke, sucking drool back into my mouth, disoriented and stiff in the darkness. A moan escaped my lips as I tried to move, but a weight on top of me kept me in place. My heart leaped into my throat, pounding as quick as my pulse. It wasn't until the block holding me down groaned that my memory flooded back. The weight lifted off me and a small flame lit the space.

"Sorry about that," Mikhail whispered and rubbed his face with his free hand.

The rest of the soldiers started stirring at the presence of light in the dark room. The heat of Mikhail along with all our bodies had turned the little space into the equivalent of a hothouse. I sat up and pulled my shirt from my sweaty skin and then wiped my face with my bandaged hand, mopping up the moisture before I hand-combed my hair and stretched. I so wished for Mikhail's shower. Perhaps we would reach his apartment building today without incident.

But I knew better. My stomach clenched as I looked around. Today was the day we'd lose some people. The streets were loaded with leviathans. The subway tunnels had been smashed by their massive feet and they were hunting us with a vengeance. After all, we took their mangled dragon instead of killing him.

I had a feeling what was left of the subway system would be swarmed with baby leviathans and now that the tunnels had massive holes in them, I was sure their screams would be heard for miles.

"What's the plan?" I asked, not really aiming it at any one in particular, but my gaze traveled from Mikhail to Troy and back, searching for an answer.

Mikhail bit his lip and glanced at our piled stash. "Douse ourselves in bleach and make a run for it. We're only a few blocks northwest of the apartment. While I would have liked to get to the closest subway station, that isn't in the cards. This is the safest location right now since we are under a building. The only other station that we'd have a prayer in would be the Trade Center, but even that could have been compromised." He looked up at the ceiling. "I don't know how bad

City Hall is up there, so we may end up with a wall of debris and have to make our way out via the tracks anyway."

"We'll still have to carry the carts," Troy said, and the sigh in his voice was clear.

I couldn't imagine their fatigue. I hadn't been one of the ones carrying the wagons along with double backpacks. I was exhausted with just my doubling of packs, and mine weren't all that heavy. The carts had to weigh at least a hundred pounds each. Although that didn't seem unsurmountable, carrying it for blocks while trying to keep an eye out for monsters was enough to make my mouth dry.

Mikhail nodded. "Rolling them on the pavement would be a recipe for disaster. Those mothers can hear anything out of the ordinary. And that's not a usual sound these days. Besides, we shouldn't try to make a run for it until it's dark. That way we will have the night in our favor."

"Can't they see at night?" Troy asked.

"Dragons can but I'm the last one left, so there's no danger in being seen anymore. Leviathans are nearly blind in the dark, but they can sniff you out from miles away. In our case, they'll be blocks away at best, so the deep shadows and narrow alleys are our best bet, even though that means it's also hard for you to see. The only thing we really have to worry about is if the leviathans get a whiff of us. If they do, it's over. Their smell receptors are scary accurate, and the only thing they actively avoid is bleach. The smell burns their noses just as badly as it burns their skin when you spray them. So, dousing in bleach is our only chance at this." He glanced at me and then my bandaged wrist. "That has to go. The smell of blood on the air will override the bleach."

I glanced down at my wrist and licked my lips. It hadn't been clean last night when he unwrapped it and I had no idea what shape it was in now. "What if I bleed through the Band-Aids?"

"We'll have to have a standoff because I can't compromise my building." He nearly winced saying the words, as if it pained him. "Let's reapply some liquid bandage and see if we can at least have enough of a buffer to keep it from seeping through."

Mikhail unwrapped my wrist and dropped the soiled bandage on the floor. Luckily, the Band-Aids seemed dry, but he still peeled them off and put a heavy amount of liquid bandage over my cuts, blowing on it until it had dried before he reapplied new Band-Aids. This time he put four on each, so it looked like I had a star patter on both the top and bottom of my wrist. Just for good measure, he added another couple on the one on the inside of my wrist and then took a step back. When he finally met my gaze, he still held that worried brow.

He took a deep breath and looked around the room. "Does anyone else have any cuts, scrapes, blisters, anything that could seep?"

Troy glanced around the room and received head shakes in response. "No," Troy said. "I'm pretty adamant about patching my team up for that same reason."

We all had seen the reaction of those things when there was fresh blood. Mikhail and I were lucky there weren't any leviathans within a few blocks of the park when we were chained to the statue by my former commander. If there had been, we both wouldn't be standing here in the midst of these soldiers.

I shook the morbid thoughts of what could have happened. Dwelling on that and not paying attention to the current crisis would likely get someone killed. We all had to be alert and cautious.

Troy maneuvered to the door and slowly opened it to the brightly lit tunnel beyond. Frigid air flowed in through the crack. He closed it as gently as possible. "We have a few hours to kill."

Jenny stood and stretched and started toward the door.

"What are you doing?" Troy asked as she reached for the knob.

"Nature calls," she said. "And this place is too small to cop a squat in the corner."

"No one goes alone." He reached for the nearest super soaker.

"I'll go with her." My bladder was feeling a bit heavy. I could use a little relief as well.

Troy hesitated before he handed me the loaded toy and then he stepped aside.

"Let the ladies have some privacy," Troy said, and I turned to see Mikhail on my heel and Troy's hand on his chest.

Mikhail's gaze snapped to Troy, and his eyes narrowed. Before he could launch into any argument, I said, "I'll be fine with Jenny."

I closed the door on his arched eyebrows. He looked like a hurt puppy.

Jenny slid around the corner and jumped down onto the track. A moment later, the sound of relief flooded the ground. When she was through, she nodded for me to do the same.

I climbed down, and almost landed in her water. I took a step to the side and lowered my pants, doing the same. It was harder to bend and balance with the healing burns on my back, but I managed not to pee on myself, so that was a win.

I finished and crawled up onto the platform. Jenny offered me a hand to help me to my feet and when we were standing close to each other, she leaned into my ear.

"The dragon cares about you a great deal," she whispered.

I frowned at her and shook my head. I was used to his nursemaid routine and although he doted on me, it was all a show. There were no feelings behind it. It was a means to an end for him.

She raised an eyebrow.

"He's a good actor," I whispered in her ear.

"If you don't want him, I'll gladly take a ride." Jenny grinned.

I blinked at her, and my mouth dropped open as an unwanted possessiveness spread through my blood. The thought of him with anyone else grated on my nerves like fingernails on a chalkboard.

Her grin remained. "Well, if you change your mind, let me know. He is a looker, and I wouldn't mind a taste." She took my hand and led me back to the room like a mother would lead a child.

Her comments threw me more than I admitted. Mikhail wasn't human. He only paired with me because I had a secret that he wanted. Once I told him what it was, he bided his time in order to destroy my platoon. If he cared about me, he never would have razed the museum. He would have found another way to neutralize my former commander.

That stubborn denial straightened my back. We slipped into the room and two other soldiers headed out to do the same. Two by two, the entire room came and went until we all looked a bit more relaxed.

I took a seat in the center where Mikhail and I had slept and rummaged through the bag I packed in the Penn Station store. I pulled out the box of sugary cereal I had confiscated. Others did the same with whatever their secret stash had been, and the quiet crunching of different dried foods filled the room. Mikhail sat down next to me. He had still been in dragon form at the time we were in that store. He picked at a hangnail on his thumb.

"Don't do that. You're likely to draw blood." I tipped the open package towards him.

He scrunched his nose at the sweet scent. "That's pure sugar."

"Fine. Starve." I went to pull the box back, but he shot his hand inside and pulled out a healthy handful, which, for his size, was nearly half the damn contents. I looked inside and then at him, both amused and irritated at the portion he took.

He gave me a crooked smile and shrugged. "Thanks," he muttered and dropped a few pieces into his mouth. He didn't grimace as he ate. As a matter of fact, he seemed to come alive with each small portion he took. When he finished, he said, "That wasn't half bad."

"You mean to tell me you've never had Crunch Berries?" They were my favorites growing up and eating them gave me a bit of nostalgia for the carefree days of just running to the store and grabbing these as a snack instead of breakfast. Although, truthfully, I could eat these for all three meals a day.

He let out a soft chuckle. "No. Meat eater. Remember?" He slid a sideways gaze in my direction that was full of humor.

"You two need to get a room," Marvin, one of the quieter soldiers, blurted.

A few others laughed at the remark and my cheeks heated. I focused on my cereal and didn't dare glance up.

"He had plenty of opportunity, but passed every time," I muttered with my mouth full. The bitterness of his rebuttal in the garage surfaced, but he had an excuse then. He had just retrieved what was left of his dead wife and kids.

"You were injured," he snapped, as if my comment hit a nerve.

I caught the glare he sent in my direction before he focused on his hands. I looked beyond him at Jenny. She waved her hand, as if saying I told you so.

His nostrils flared and he forced himself to meet my gaze. Fire burned in his irises, but it wasn't an inferno like his eyes had reflected back at the apartment just before he bolted away and shifted into dragon form. This was a slow burn.

"It's called transference." I rolled up the interior cereal bag so what was left wouldn't go stale and stuffed the bag back into my backpack.

"I'm not so sure," he said under his breath, stood up, and headed to the door. He cracked it and scanned the tunnel before closing it. He shuffled his feet and glanced around the room.

Everyone had smirks that I wanted to wipe from their faces. From the look on Mikhail's face, he shared my unhappiness in their demeanor.

"Give it a rest. We have more important things to focus on right now," Troy said from near the back. His gaze pierced through me as if he were trying to figure me out. "Where are we headed exactly, in case we get separated?"

"Water Street. Near Fulton."

Mikhail surprised me by answering the question. But he did not expand with a number or an exact location.

"If we get separated, I will circle back to find you," Mikhail added.

"We'll carry the bleach," Troy said, reading into the unsaid statement in the same way I had. Mikhail was all about self-preservation and if that meant he had to desert us, he would.

"I'll carry her." He pointed at me as if I were as precious a cargo as the bins of bleach.

"I can walk on my own," I snapped. I was not a bargaining chip or something to be claimed. And I certainly was not Mikhail's pawn.

"Fine," Mikhail said in a way that was anything but fine. Aggravation lines framed the sides of his lips as he glared at me as if I had ruined some underlying agenda.

We weren't alone, so I couldn't just blurt out *what the fuck is wrong with you* in front of all these relative strangers. But I did my best to convey it with my expression. Although I knew it was a long shot, I wanted everyone here to make it to Mikhail's place without harm.

"You can carry me if you'd like," Jenny offered, pulling Mikhail's sharp gaze in her direction.

"Are you injured?" he asked.

"No," Jenny answered. "But the idea of being carried by someone so..." She fanned herself with her hand.

"She is still healing from the burns and from the spikes that were shoved into her wrists. If she gets into a high-stress situation, her blood pressure will rise, and those bandages may not hold back her blood." His gaze swung back to me. "I wasn't offering to carry you out of some sense of misplaced machoism. I was offering to carry you to spare all of us the possibility of being detected."

I blinked at his venomous outburst. "Oh." I didn't quite know what else to say. I did not wish to be carried like an invalid, but he had a point. "I guess if that's your reasoning, I'm not as offended by the offer." I stumbled on my words.

"You can walk until it becomes dangerous," he said. "Then I'm hauling you over my shoulder and getting you somewhere that they cannot sense you. Understand? If I smell blood, they can smell blood, and that puts all of us in danger."

The realization I could put the team in jeopardy slid over my skin like a dead fish. "Then why don't you leave me here? If I'm going to put the mission in danger, I shouldn't go."

This time he balked at me, as if that wasn't even an option. "You've never left anyone behind. Why the hell should I?"

"I agree with the dragon," Troy said. "We do not leave people behind. Ever."

It was my turn to use that dreaded word that means things are not copasetic. "Fine." I put my hands up in surrender and then turned away from the men making the decisions for the rest of us. I caught Jenny's gaze and gave her a raised eyebrow, communicating that I told her so. He wasn't into me. He was only into safeguarding his own ass.

12

Nightfall couldn't come fast enough. All of us were getting antsy and short in the small confines of the room. Sunset couldn't have come at a better time. And now that the tunnel was painted in darkness, we used the spray bottle on mist and sprayed each one of us down from crown to toe with it. It took two whole bottles to mist us into leviathan invisibility, and even my nose was burning from being in the small space full of bleach fumes.

We filed out with the bins of bleach, shuffling along the ramp as if any noise would bring a swarm of deadly monsters. I held my super soaker at the ready, even though all I could see were shadows. Mikhail's heat swathed over me like a security blanket, and he might as well have his hand on my back, leading me through the maze that led to City Hall. I wanted to shuffle faster, put more distance between us right now, but we were leading the pack and if I didn't keep up, he'd just haul me over his shoulder.

At least he had my back. But did he have everyone else's?

That thought burrowed under my skin and I tried to shake it. I needed to focus on what lay ahead even though on first look, all that enveloped us was blackness of a building that hadn't had running electricity for years and possibly had been crushed by leviathan feet or burned out by dragon flame. As soon as we reached the top of the ramp, there wasn't a clear pathway to follow.

Mikhail sparked flames from his fingers to get our bearings. The brightness of the light made me squint. We were in a small vestibule, barely as big as the storeroom we had rested in. A door with a stairway sign on it stood at the far side of the room and a separate door stood in front of us.

"Why'd you stop?" I whispered.

"I think this brings us into the lobby and the stairs bring us to the upper floors, but I don't remember." Mikhail glanced between the two doors. "We don't want to go to the upper floors, and we certainly don't want to go out the main entrance with that tall staircase that will leave us utterly exposed. We want a street exit, preferably in back.”

“And we don’t want to go up the wrong staircase that opens to that little building on the east side of the little park,” Troy said from behind us.

“That would actually be better than the front stairwell. At least there we wouldn’t be easily seen. Dark figures on the white stairs are easy to spot, even with crappy vision.”

“Make a choice. These bins aren’t getting any lighter.” Troy’s voice carried some of the strain visible in his arms and neck.

Mikhail glanced at the far door with the stairwell icon tattooed into the steel and turned back to the door in front of him. He twisted the knob and pulled. Nothing happened. The door did not budge. He used a little more force and it groaned in protest.

“Is it unlocked?” I asked as my brain seized the fact that Mikhail’s strength wasn’t enough to move the door. Even with it swinging out as opposed to in.

“The knob moves easily, but...” He put both hands on the doorknob.

“Back away,” I said as silent alarms went off in my head. I pulled his hands away from the handle and pushed him back as my mind raced.

"What is your issue?" He tried to get around me.

"I think it's booby-trapped precisely for someone like you." I turned and met Troy's gaze. "Shit. This is exactly the kind of place Yoman spoke of. Did you ever meet Yoman? I don't know which platoon he was with, but he bragged one night about setting up the monsters if they ever did get into the tunnels."

"Yoman was a drunk," one of the soldiers toward the back said.

"Yes, but he was brilliant with explosives." I had seen him take down a couple of buildings trying to take out leviathans. Of course, this was before we found out bleach made them vulnerable. He got away in the dust the rubble kicked up, but all it had done was aggravate the leviathans.

"You mean psychotic," Troy said. "He was certifiable. Blew himself up to try to take out a group of leviathans. This was before we knew about bleach." He looked around at both doors. "Damn it." He closed his eyes tight as if he were trying to pull out a memory, but he just shook his head.

I had wondered what had happened to him, but Troy was not wrong. Yoman was certifiable near the end.

"I remember that fool." Mikhail spoke softly as he eyed the door. "If Holly is right, a blast like what he created when he died will take down this building." He doused the fire in his hand, plunging us into the dark. "Fuck."

The way he drew out the word sent a rash of gooseflesh over my skin and made me wish that he would whisper that in my ear, but under vastly different circumstances. I dismissed the thought with a wave of my hand.

He's a dragon. I'm human. Nothing we do would work, regardless of the fact he had a human wife before.

Man, I needed to get laid so this string of thoughts would fade away. It had been forever since I had been with someone and that was probably why my mind kept wandering into the gutter instead of focusing on the danger surrounding us.

"It looks like we have no choice but to find our way out through the tracks," Troy said with a heavy sigh.

"Fuck that. Why don't we try the stairwell? We can always circle back down from the second floor," one of the male soldier's said. And their voice got farther away as he spoke, along with the squeak of wheels rolling across the floor.

Mikhail lit his fingers again just as Diego reached for the door.

"No!" I called louder than I meant to, and Mikhail spread his arms and pushed the rest of us back down the ramp with four of the five carts. He shifted into dragon form to move all of us and our shopping carts down and onto the subway tracks.

The explosion rocked the building, dropping dust on top of us. Mikhail didn't stop at the entry, but pushed us back as far as our bleach line. Protecting us from the initial explosion. He shifted back to human and hauled me over his shoulder.

"Run!" he ordered and jogged away from the station.

We were only what would have been less than a block away from the building when the secondary explosion triggered. This one not only dropped tiles onto us, but the already compromised tunnel seemed to collapse all around us.

The soldiers pushed the carts instead of carrying them as they ran. We got to a platform and stopped for a moment to collect our breaths. This was the Broadway City Hall platform. And I did not want to be this close to the destruction.

"Lower tracks," I hissed.

Mikhail slowed for a moment and hopped up on the platform, helping the others. He seemed to understand my request, and led the group down into the bowels of the tunnels. This area had a lower level that had been meant for the express trains, but it was unfinished. The gate to the lower level was locked, but one kick from Mikhail, and the metal gave. He caught it before it crashed into the stairway and then stepped aside so the team could bring our stash down. Then he pushed the door closed again, attempting to reengage whatever had kept it closed before.

The sounds of a super soaker dousing the entry filled my ears and then Mikhail lit his fingers, letting a soft glow lead the way. He took the southwest tunnel, making his way slowly and carefully as the team followed. Now that we weren't running, the soldiers carried the carts.

"You can put me down now," I said as I bounced on Mikhail's shoulder, making each word come out in a huff of air.

"Oh. Right." He gently set me on my feet. "I don't' know if we can get out of here with our carts. We might need to leave them somewhere and only bring what we can carry. Then, once we figure out their patrol patterns, we can do a couple retrieval missions to get the rest."

He wiped his face with his free hand.

I didn't like the sound of his plan, but before I could speak, Troy chimed in.

"That's the only path in, isn't it?" Troy hooked his thumb back the way we came. Troy's face was pale and his eyes held a haunted quality, like he was just coming to terms with what happened.

I did a quick head count. We were short more than just Diego.

"Where's Jenny?" I liked having another female on the team, even if she did have the hots for Mikhail.

"She and Karl went after Diego just before your boy swept us down to the tunnel with his wings."

"Why?" I couldn't help the question. My brain had stalled when I saw Diego heading for what I had already deemed the danger zone.

He shrugged. "I would have gone after him myself, but I didn't get the chance." This time he leveled a glare at Mikhail, as though he had been the one to trigger the bomb that killed three of his soldiers. He put the bin down and stepped forward, fisting his hands.

I stepped between them, putting my palms on Troy's chest to keep him from doing something that would result in Mikhail losing his temper. I had seen what a single punch from an angry dragon could do. Troy's heart hammered against my splayed fingers.

"He was trying to protect us." I used the softest voice I could to try to defuse whatever he had in mind. Based on the beat of his heart and the glare in his eyes, he wanted to deliver a big dose of whoop-ass. But right now, that would further delay us from safety.

Troy looked down at me and then my hands on his chest.

"I don't need you stepping in," he snarled and grabbed my wrists, forcibly removing them from his body.

I hissed as he squeezed my injuries. Before I could react, Mikhail's hand shot out and closed around Troy's throat. Troy released me and his eyes widened at Mikhail.

"You dare hurt her?" Mikhail growled in a way that promised death.

"Let him go, Mikhail. He's just lost three of his own people. He did not intend to hurt me," I snapped as I spun to face him. The look in his eyes told me reason was not going to work in this instance. "Stop this bullshit," I ordered in a snarl. "Both of you. Otherwise, we will not make it out of here alive."

I wasn't sure whether it was my tone or my words, but Mikhail slowly released Troy's neck. "I am sorry you lost some of your people." He stepped back. "But if you harm Sergeant Woods ever again, it will be the last thing you do."

Troy held the glare for a moment longer and then looked down at me. "I did not intend to hurt you."

I couldn't tell whether he was sincere or not, but it didn't matter. I just wanted the safety of Mikhail's building right now and not the bullshit of high emotions that we were all experiencing.

"I know. Now can we please move on?" I waved in the direction we were headed before Mikhail had put me down. Instead of waiting for a response, I took it upon myself to lead this not-so-merry little band of ours and marched ahead.

"She sure is a pistol," Troy mumbled, loud enough for me to hear.

"You have no idea," Mikhail replied, and then their footfalls began.

I didn't bother looking over my shoulder until I came to a fork in the unfinished tunnel. Both avenues were dark and neither gave me any indication of direction. Mikhail stepped to one side and Troy the other, both with the same perplexed expression I was sure I sported.

"Which way?" I asked, trying to remember all I had read about these old, unfinished tunnels.

"One leads to a dead end, the other will gradually narrow down to nothing," Mikhail said.

"So, both are dead ends," Troy said.

"That's what it sounds like to me." I glanced at Mikhail. "Which way?"

"We want the dead end because there's an exit that goes up to the street level. I don't think there's any exits in the one that narrows down to nothing because it's under the current tunnel." He studied both openings and shook his head. "You choose."

I sighed and did a silent eenie, meeny, miny, moe and ended up choosing the left tunnel despite ending on the right side. I always went against the grain, and it had worked out for me for the most part.

It wasn't until we went the equivalent of a few city blocks that the ceiling felt as if it were sinking closer to us. I slowed and glanced at it and then over at Mikhail.

We went another block and the slope in the ceiling became evident. I chose the wrong path. I slowed to a stop; so did the men following with the carts in their grasp.

"We need to go back and take the other path," I said, owning the mistake.

A few groaned, but they let us move to the back of the line and lead the way. I wondered just how much their arms and backs would be hurting once we got somewhere we all could rest without the fear of what was around the next corner. Guilt bit at the edges of my mind. The only saving grace for us was there were no baby leviathans on this level as the only entry was the one we came down and none of it had our signatures on it. Plus, the bleach Mikhail had sprayed would deter them from climbing down the stairs.

We made quick work of backtracking and once headed in the right direction, we made our way until the tunnel just ended. The men put down their loads and leaned against the walls, stretching their arms.

Mikhail grabbed a bottle of bleach out of a cart and walked a few paces back, laying down a line of the liquid across the tunnel. He emptied the bottle in the process and then set it down on the other side of the line before he came back to us.

"What's that for?" Troy asked.

"Protection." Mikhail glanced around the tunnel and sighed. There wasn't a formal exit like we had seen in several places between stations on our journey. Instead, there only seemed to be dirt-caked walls. Mikhail started at one end and walked, with his fingers dragging on the wall. He stopped at one point and then wiped his hand across the wall, wiping dirt off a dark metal door. There was no doorknob but his slow progress of clearing the dirt away revealed a hole where a knob should be. He lightly clapped his hands to rid them of the dirt and grime he had cleared and then he reached into the hole. With the meat of his palm on the door, he slowly pushed.

The hinges creaked loud enough for me to understand his preparation with the line of bleach. If any baby leviathans were loose in the tunnels, that high-pitched whine would bring them forth despite the bleach barriers. Once Mikhail had the door wide, he waved the crew inside the cramped space. A metal staircase looped back and forth up at least three stories.

Once we were all squished inside, he closed the door. That loud squeak radiated through the concrete room we stood in, and everyone froze in place.

"Take a load off for a bit," Mikhail whispered. The men pushed the carts into the corner under the stairs and found places to sit on the steps. Mikhail climbed the stairs and I followed, with Troy at my heels.

"I hope the doors up top don't make a ruckus like the door below," Mikhail said softly. "Otherwise, we are dead."

"We should probably catch some rest here before we try to carry those carts up these stairs," Troy said as we continued our ascent in the stuffy stairwell.

We passed by another landing with an exterior door. This one had a doorknob and a designated railway path for the 2 and 3 lines. Mikhail pressed his finger to his lips, and we slid by the entrance of the subway tunnel. The higher we reached, the more natural light bathed the stairwell. We rounded the last corner and paused. Mikhail closed his fist, dousing the fire that had led us up most of the stairs.

The exit was warped and indented, but it didn't look like it was done by a leviathan foot. No, this looked more like a building toppled onto the exit. However, light still filtered through the crack.

Mikhail ran his hand through his hair and took a seat on the stairs in a defeated posture. I opened my mouth, but he shook his head and put his finger to his lips again. He pointed down the stairs more emphatically, but as we started down, he didn't follow.

I hesitated and then waved Troy down and climbed back up. Mikhail had his head down, his elbows on his knees and his palms propping his head up. He didn't look up at me when I stepped into his field of view.

"I've failed you," he whispered, and my heart nearly stopped.

I knelt and pulled his hands away from his face until he met my gaze. I couldn't have him thinking he failed me—or humanity, for that matter. I searched his defeated gaze and shook my head.

"I can't open that. If I do, we're likely to be smothered by debris." He pointed above him.

I glanced up and weighed his words. "But there is light coming through." I brought my gaze to his. "So, there is a path out, however harrowing it may be."

He reached out and cupped my cheek, running his thumb along my skin. It was something a lover would do, and it created a web of sensations through me that spread like a warm blanket. But the four words that fell from his lips chilled me to the core.

"It will make noise."

My heart sank. Noise meant the monsters would come in droves.

13

We gathered on the ground floor. Mikhail stared at the ground without making eye contact with anyone. It was as if he were trying to pull the right words to explain our situation. Instead of letting him struggle through it, I cleared my throat.

"It seems that there is building debris on the exit," I said quietly.

Faces fell, so did whatever hope reflected in their eyes.

"But there is light coming through," Troy said as he waved up the stairwell, as if that would change the truth.

"Yes. But opening those doors will make a lot of noise and I don't know how much of it will fall into the stairwell." Mikhail met Troy's gaze.

Troy bit his lower lip. "Aren't buildings collapsing here and there anyway from the damage you did?" He cocked his head in a challenge.

Mikhail stared at him and nodded, but didn't react to the dig. He traded a glance with me before he asked, "Are you willing to risk being buried alive?"

Troy studied the ground with his lower lip sucked between his teeth and his brow creased in thought. It took him a good five minutes of internal debate before he spoke. "The alternative is going back through the subway system, and we all know that's been compromised. The likelihood of us reaching our destination going that route is slim." He took a breath and then met Mikhail's gaze head on. "So, yes. I think we'd rather risk being buried alive if it means we have a chance of defeating them in the end. Pour bleach all over the landing up there and then open it up. Let them come investigate. We will wait it out down here and when night falls, we'll attempt to climb out. If we can't, then we'll be forced to backtrack."

The rest of the soldiers nodded. "We agree," a few of them piped in softly.

Mikhail glanced at me and licked his lips. "It's dangerous for everyone here, including me." He stared into my eyes, trying to transmit his thoughts on the matter visually. "But I'll attempt it if you agree it's the right course of action."

The fact he didn't frame it as a question made me shift my weight. I knew he wasn't convinced this was the right route to take just by his non-question, but I couldn't see any other way out. And if anyone could survive having a building fall on him, it was Mikhail. No one else in this stairwell had the strength to open the door. I slowly nodded. "I'd not only douse that landing, but the stairs leading down to deter any sort of investigation. But other than that, I agree that it is our best chance," I answered. "Just don't get cut," I added and squeezed his hand.

Mikhail gave me an uneasy smile. "I'll try not to." He glanced around and sighed. "Just stay put." He grabbed a couple of bottles of bleach and headed up the stairs.

We piled back under the stairwell next to the door to the subway tunnel and waited. The stench of bleach filled the space and then the ripping of metal echoed off the walls, followed by such a racket that we covered our ears. Dust mingled with bleach fumes.

My heart thundered as silence settled. Mikhail didn't come down the stairs like I thought he would. The ground around us shook. The need to run up to make sure he was all right gripped me, and I moved toward the stairs.

Troy grabbed my arm and shook his head, as if he read my thoughts. He put his finger to his lips as well and pulled me deeper into the alcove with the rest of the soldiers and our bins of bleach.

Of course, Troy was right. If I went running blind up the stairs, I'd compromise everyone, including Mikhail if he was okay. If he wasn't, we'd eventually dig him out and get him to his apartment building. I just hoped he was alive and stayed that way.

Even so, Troy kept his grip on me, as if he didn't trust me to make the right decision. I tried to shake his hand off, but he kept it solid as he glanced up at the ceiling above us. The concrete held. Even with our flashlights out, I could see the fear in his eyes.

"Another building collapse?" the gravelly voice of the Serpent King echoed from the street level.

"Looks that way," another said in a ghastly voice that I never heard before. I had to assume that was a leviathan speaking, although they had never spoken English before. I'd only heard the hideous hissing noises from them. But then again, they were usually doused with bleach.

"Can you detect any traces of blood like the other collapses?"

Sniffing, followed by a cough. "No, sir," the pained voice said. "No blood, but that stench that burns my nose is present."

Silence followed, as if the monsters were considering the presence of bleach as a sign of some sort. And then the Serpent King's voice asked, "Have you ever smelled that with other collapses?"

"Yes, sir. In some buildings, but not others."

"And the buildings that you have smelled it, have you also smelled blood?"

I raised an eyebrow and met Troy's gaze. He just shrugged. But at least there was no smell of blood, which meant Mikhail was not bleeding at all. Or if he was, it wasn't significant enough to overpower the bleach. Yet.

"Some yes, some no. There's no discernable pattern."

More silence as the rubble shifted and more bricks tumbled down the stairs.

"I want a few of you to watch the building. If anything tries to escape, crush it." The order came through loud and clear.

We would have to wait out their watch, which meant we wouldn't be able to get to Mikhail any time soon. I didn't know what shape the rest of the stairwell was in or what the debris above ground looked like either. Thankfully, we had food and water to last at least another day before we'd have to figure out something more permanent.

The presence of leviathans also meant no light that might bleed out from the rubble, and no speaking until we had a chance to escape this deathtrap.

After a few minutes of quiet shuffling above, it seemed the sentries found their guard spots. I peeled Troy's hand off my arm and signed to him that I was going to check the stairs. He glanced at his men and then nodded with a signal for me to be very, very quiet.

I did not climb to my feet. Using my hands and knees made only a whisper of noise on the steps versus the footfalls that my boots would have made no matter how quiet I wanted to be. Two flights went without a piece of the building above visible despite the dust hanging on the air like an unwanted fog.

It tickled my nose, and I clamped down on both my nose and my mouth, stopping the need to sneeze. As the tingle abated, I blinked back the latent tears leftover from the close call. Light filtered in much more readily as I climbed the steps to the third-floor landing. There was enough brick and glass to slow my ascent. I didn't need to cut my hands or knees on what was strewn all over the ground. I moved far enough to take a glance around the corner and up the stairwell.

My throat tightened. Mikhail was partly lying out of the rubble down the steps. The metal door covered him from the brunt of the ruins, but he now seemed trapped under that same sheet of metal and he was not conscious. A large bump marred his forehead, as if the metal jarred into him and knocked him out. He was lucky it didn't split his head open. I gently brushed the scraps of glass away from the path in front of me and slowly moved toward him, mindful of the dangers above.

As I climbed closer, his eyes blinked open, darting around as if he had no idea what had happened. At least he had the wherewithal to not make noise. When his gaze landed on me, his eyes widened. I put my finger to my lips, using the same silence gesture he had, and then pointed above and made claws out of both hands to signify monsters were up there.

His brow knit and his lips thinned, and he jabbed his jaw in the direction of the stairs. He was trying to tell me to get out of there, but I took another step closer, ultra-aware that around the corner there was a pile of building wreckage blocking the stairwell and beyond that, some leviathans waited for any sign of life.

I shook my head. I was not leaving him.

"Go," he mouthed.

"No one left behind," I mouthed slowly, making my point without words.

He closed his eyes and shook his head before he laid it back on the concrete. Wincing, he pulled his arm out from behind the rubble and pointed down the stairs. When his eyes opened, they were in his inferno mode, which meant I needed to heed his warning.

I slowly traced my way back down to the landing. But I really didn't want to slip around the corner. I wanted him within view. Something inside me balked when he pointed again, especially because it came with another grimace. But I had to trust him, trust that he was not mortally wounded and wouldn't slip away while we waited the monsters out. I moved slowly out of his view and then leaned on the wall with a frustrated exhale.

I stood in place for roughly ten minutes and then peeked around the corner. Mikhail was attempting to pull himself out from under the rubble without shifting the debris. Sweat dripped from his face onto the stair. At least I thought it was sweat, until he happened to glance in my direction.

My jaw slackened. It wasn't sweat but tears. His face was as red as a tomato. Ignoring his silent plea, I nearly ran up the stairs despite the shake of his head. I swept the glass aside with my boot and knelt, cradling his head in my lap.

His hand shook as he signed for me to leave.

"No," I whispered in his ear. "What can I do?"

He shook his head and used his hand to communicate letters slowly. "I am broken," he signed.

I blinked and my gaze met his; I repeated the letters representing broken to make sure I understood what the hell he was saying.

He nodded. "Can not feel legs," he signed.

I slumped against the wall and wiped my face. "We'll figure it out," I signed. "We have enough carts to carry you."

He shook his head. "Leave me."

"We need you. You have the knowledge to build the bomb and the fire to destroy the leviathan's once the bomb goes off," I signed slowly.

He closed his eyes. "I don't think I'll be able to fly, which is the most efficient way of destroying them."

"Then we figure out another way. Hell, I can push you through the masses while you torch those fuckers if I have to."

That earned me a tilted smile. I took his free hand in mine and ran my fingers through his hair while I stretched out on the stair below him. We couldn't attempt to move the metal pinning him yet. I also didn't want to try to pull him out and break open skin. The smell of dragon blood would be our demise, even more than human blood.

A small noise below made me turn my head. Troy was at the base of the stairs. I gave him a shrug and signed, "Mikhail is hurt."

His gaze went to the head buried in my lap and then met mine. "How bad?"

"He can't feel his legs," I signed.

Troy closed his eyes and then started up the stairs.

Mikhail lifted his head and put his hand out in a stop signal.

Troy obeyed.

"Not yet. Wait until dark. Otherwise, they will attack," Mikhail signed. "They may still attack in the dark, but at least they won't have clear targets."

Troy nodded. He pulled out a bottle of water and offered it to me. I reached out and he came far enough to hand it to me, his steps only a whisper that couldn't be heard above the creaking of some of the debris. He also put a spray bottle on the stair below me.

"Thank you," I signed.

"Any time," he replied with his hands. "See you at dusk."

I gave him a thumbs-up and then opened the water, taking a small sip before offering Mikhail the bottle. He took a small sip, but some of it landed on my pants below him. He capped the bottle and handed it to me before laying his head on his arm across my legs.

I resumed hand-combing his hair gently. It was as silky as I thought it would be, and the slow motion lulled him into the even breathing of sleep. As I stared down at his profile, I let my mind flow over everything that had happened between us. It wasn't transference that tightened my throat.

This was truly the first time I had to reflect on this pressure in my chest. To examine my feelings and identify them as true. Despair raked through me as I realized I was falling in love with one of the monsters that had declared war on the human race.

14

As the light began to fade, those horrid voices came from above, making me stiffen in place.

"Has there been any sign of life?"

"None. Not even rodents fleeing the rubble. There have been shifts in the debris, so don't get too close."

"We'll stay clear. You're relieved for the night."

"Try not to fall asleep from boredom."

A snicker followed and then feet pounded away. It wasn't too long before we heard snoring from above. The idiots fell asleep.

I glanced down at Mikhail. At least he hadn't snored in his fitful sleep. I glanced at the shadows in the stairwell below and as if I had called out loud, Troy slid into view with a couple of soldiers behind him. They made their way carefully up the stairs. In the darkening space, they inspected the metal holding Mikhail pinned on the landing.

Mikhail jerked awake, and I palmed his cheek as I slid out from under him. I sprayed us all down with the bleach and sprayed the debris above Mikhail as well. Whatever they were planning to do would shift things and I didn't want the monsters deciding to put a foot into the hole and effectively crushing us. Any shift would send a plume of bleach scent upward and hopefully that would be enough of a deterrent.

Troy tapped me on the shoulder and mimed me pulling. He snapped his finger and Adam, another one of Troy's soldiers, came up the stairs behind me, just in case Mikhail came out faster than we anticipated. It wouldn't do for us to tumble down the steps, so Adam stood behind me with his palms bracing my lower back.

I maneuvered enough to get my hands under Mikhail's arms. He laid his head on my shoulder and grit his teeth. He wrapped his arms over mine, understanding that he wasn't going to be able to stop this rescue operation.

I glanced at him, and he gave me a small nod, although he looked much paler than he had when I first saw him. I, in turn, nodded at Troy.

Troy counted down with his fingers and then the three lifted the metal door from the end closest to the stairs. They tried to keep it level, too. A feat that I marveled at until Troy nodded at me.

I pulled Mikhail. He shifted more out of the debris but then it seemed as if he caught on something. He arched and hissed between closed lips. I saw what was preventing me from pulling him out and put him on the stairs and pointed at Adam behind me, silently instructing him to take my place.

He did, without hesitation.

I crawled into the space over Mikhail, praying that Troy and the other two could sustain holding the door. If not, I'd be crushed under the weight. Even so, I braced my back against the metal and gripped the concrete cylinder that had Mikhail's right leg pinned. I barely moved it the first try. If I could make noise, it would have been better, but the next try, I got it high enough to see the damage.

Mikhail would probably never walk again, but what was more concerning was the fact his calf was not a bloody pulp. Instead, it looked like a mass of purple, as though his skin was all that held in the crushed bone and mangled blood vessels.

Adam pulled and Mikhail's leg released. I crawled backward as fast as Adam dragged

Mikhail free, and then Troy and the other two lowered the metal door as gracefully as possible. The debris groaned and shifted again, sending a few bricks crumbling down the steps as we carried Mikhail into the safety of the darkness below.

When we reached the bottom of the stairs, we passed through a heavy blanket that had been hung, blocking out light and dust from above. It also made the space below as dark as a cloudless night in the sticks. When the flashlights went on, we all squinted.

My eyes adjusted fairly quickly, and when the soldiers set Mikhail on his side, I winced. Just one good look at his leg was enough.

"His leg needs to be amputated," Troy said, softly enough for me to almost miss it.

I could not fathom cutting him open here in this stairwell.

Mikhail was already shaking his head.

"They'll smell dragon blood, even through the bleach," I said quietly. "We have to get him to his apartment building. Then we can do whatever surgery is necessary."

Mikhail pointed at me and nodded, and then his eyes slipped closed. Tears leaked out of the side of his eyes and his teeth grit together as sweat formed on his forehead. His nails began to form the familiar claws. Mikhail was shifting.

I pushed people aside because I did not know whether he could contain his form or whether a full-fledged dragon was going to transform in front of us or whether he was just shifting into the mini-dragon he had been throughout most of this little band's travels.

A full dragon in this cramped space would crush us all to death.

Mikhail's eyes flashed open with a citrine glow and that reptilian shape. His teeth elongated and he met my gaze. Concern flashed across his features just before they morphed. Somehow, he contained his agony as bones popped out of place and then rearranged. Iridescent scales seemed to pop out of his skin, covering every inch of his form, including his mangled leg.

He remained in his human size, but even with the transformation, he didn't seem to be able to move from his spot on the ground. Without prompting from anyone, he closed his eyes again. This time, he shrank his form smaller than before, arching in torment until he finally collapsed in a heap on the floor. His breathing sounded labored, and I leaned over, scooping him into my arms.

He released a small hiss but then settled into my arms, wrapping his wings around himself as if he were a tiny child in need of comfort. I glanced at Troy and Adam and the others who had witnessed this insanity.

"We need to take only what we can carry. If he was right on the location, I can get us to the apartment building. Just make sure you have those super soakers loaded up and at the ready. If we run into trouble, then we'll have to start shooting because I don't know if Mik has enough energy to spare us a fire." I was glad my voice remained calm, without any of the panic pounding my muscles straight to the bone.

"Will he heal like that?" Troy whispered and pointed.

I couldn't tell whether the lilt in his voice was wishful thinking or something else. I didn't bother clarifying because I didn't have a concrete answer for him. I just shrugged. Mikhail's chest already rose and fell in that even cadence of sleep. He needed rest if he had any hope of healing. But I didn't know whether sleep would be enough. Not with his declaration that he was broken and didn't think he'd be able to fly. His wings seemed fine to me, but then again, I'd never been a dragon, so I didn't know about the complexities of his spinal structure.

As the six soldiers packed what bleach they could carry in their backpacks, I kept Mikhail safely tucked in my arms.

Troy turned with a fully loaded backpack, and he helped me slide it on without jostling Mikhail.

He clipped it around my waist and above my chest and then tightened it.

I winced but kept Mikhail as still as possible despite the weight pulling me backward. I adjusted my stance, so I was more hunched over Mikhail and the pack settled easier on my back.

I made sure Mikhail was protected by my arms, and I'd keep him nestled as comfortably as I could until we reached his door.

If we reached the building.

All I knew is we had to try, especially since Bozo One and Bozo Two up top were sleeping. That could allow us to sneak away into the dark without being seen. And once we were in Mikhail's apartment building, we'd have to assess whether what we had was enough to do sustainable damage to the leviathans.

If it wasn't enough, then we'd have to figure out a viable recovery mission for the rest of our resources left in this stairwell.

15

We traded the food, water, and clothes in our backpacks with bottles of bleach. Between the remaining seven of us, we were able to get a little more than one of the biggest carts of bleach packed away and still be nimble on our feet. Once we finished, all lights were extinguished. One by one, we made our way beyond the blanket. The stairwell had gone from having ambient light to pitch dark as we climbed, with Troy in the front and me right behind him.

I held his belt loop and in turn, Adam held mine, and so on down the line. I was the only one not equipped with a super soaker at the ready. Mine hung on my back because with Mikhail nestled in my arm, I had no way to wield the gun.

Without the aid of lights, climbing the mountain of rubble was challenging to say the least. Each step needed to be tested to make sure it could bear our weight. So, the trek was slow as each of us followed Troy as best we could in the dark. When we broke through the surface, a sliver of a moon gave us enough visibility to see the sleeping leviathans. They had taken up residence in the street, blocking both the north and south exits. We wanted to go east, so we shuffled along the edge of the buildings until we came to the alley between them.

Our visibility was fleeting as clouds moved over the only light in the sky, hiding the moon behind them.

We did not know whether we were going down a dead end, or whether it would open up on the next avenue, but we had to take the only immediate path available to us and pray it would work.

One of the leviathans huffed and we all froze, holding our breaths while pointing the soakers at the alley entrance. When the snores resumed, we collectively let the air out of our lungs and continued our slow progression deeper into the darkness.

My arms ached from the weight of Mikhail. Even in this little package he surrendered to, he was not a light load to carry. Twenty pounds of dead weight felt like concrete in my arms. I couldn't imagine trying to carry his two-hundred-pound human form. As it was, we were slower with the bleach load we carried, and I wasn't sure we would have made it out of that stairwell with Mikhail over someone's shoulder.

Troy stopped in front of me, and my wandering mind snapped back to the present. I put my hand back to stop Adam from plowing into both of us. He did the same until the end of the line.

"Fuck."

The muttered swear was loud enough for me to pick it up and I prayed it didn't echo down the alley to where the sleeping monsters would hear.

Mikhail didn't stir.

Troy moved to the right slowly, as if feeling his way along whatever barrier he had encountered.

I tilted my head back and I saw nothing. No stars, no moon. Nothing, which meant either we were under some sort of overhang, or tonight's cloud cover had thickened.

Rain would be our worst enemy. It would dilute the bleach and reveal our scent. My heart jumped into my throat at that thought. Especially if we had indeed hit a dead end. There was no place to hide once that happened. Our bleach would be ineffective, and we had too many streets to cross to get to the apartment.

As if God thought it was great fun to challenge us in such a way, a drop hit my forehead. But no others followed. However, the sticky, heavy air of a foggy mist wrapped around us. It was still dangerous, but at least it wasn't a soaking rain. But still, prolonged exposure to this mist would eventually render the bleach we sprayed on ourselves useless.

Troy understood the dangers as well. He moved quicker, trying to find a viable way out. When he hit another barricade to the right, his muttered curse wasn't as audible. He backtracked and the team followed like a centipede turning on its axis.

This time he found a passage on the left side, and after a few steps, it jogged to the right. When it jogged left again, my senses flared. I was sure this was taking us away from where we needed to be. When we veered right again, I began to think the labyrinth we were in was a twisted maze meant to disorient.

It wasn't until we stepped out onto a street that we halted. The white letters on the sign nearly made me cry with relief. We were on Pearl Street, which meant the apartment wasn't as far as I had anticipated. But without seeing the nearest cross street, I wasn't sure which direction to take.

Our eyes adjusted to the more open lane before us, and I took Troy's hand, spelling out the most pressing question.

"What's the nearest cross street?"

He pushed me back into the alley, along with the rest of the soldier train and then spelled out "Wait here" with his fingers.

I patted Adam's hand holding my belt twice, which meant to hold tight. I breathed slowly in through my nose and out through my mouth, calming my pounding heart.

When Troy blocked the exit, I jerked. Thankfully, I did not yelp. He took my free hand and signed, "Maiden to our left."

I nodded and mentally pictured the map of downtown in my head. If I calculated right, we only had two short blocks before we got to Mikhail's building. There had to be multiple ways to enter but I only knew of the Water Street entrance.

"Any signs of patrols?"

"No."

I needed to wake Mikhail before we made a run for it. He was the only one with the building code to get us inside, and I could not chance waking him up at the last minute. I stepped back, giving Troy a chance to squeeze back into the narrow walkway we stood in.

I leaned close to the dragon's ear. "Mikhail," I whispered and gently jostled him in my arms.

Nothing happened. No startle. No eyes suddenly glowing in the dark. No reaction from the dragon in my arms. My heart thundered at the lack of response, and I held his chest to my ear, holding my breath.

His heart was still beating, and I closed my eyes as a wave of relief nearly cut me off at the knees.

"Mikhail," I said a little louder and shook him a little more vigorously.

I bit my lip. Instead of repeating my actions, I pressed my lips to his cheek and whispered his name in his ear like a lover would. I kept the mounting panic from my voice, but if he had any level of consciousness, he'd feel my runaway pulse. The smallest of citrine light flashed before it fell into dark again.

"Wake up," I whispered in the same seductively sly way I imagined men liked. That drummed up a sigh from his form. "I need you," I continued, whispering in his ear low enough so no one else but him could hear.

This time when his eyes fluttered open, they stayed open and focused on me as if I were a stranger. He blinked a few times and then tried to move, and his eyes squeezed closed as his teeth gnashed for a moment.

"Woods?" he said just as softly, as though he sensed the danger around us.

"Yes," I whispered in his ear. "We are a block away from the northwest side of your building. Is there an entrance on this side?"

He shook his head slowly. "Three-five-two-seven-six-one," he whispered and closed his eyes. "And wait until the patrol goes by before making a break for the door. That will give you a ten-minute window."

I nodded and cataloged the number sequence he just gave me, wondering what the significance of the numbers were. I would bet my life that was his passcode to get into the building and they were dates that meant something to Mikhail. Without the passcode, the only other way into the building was with Mikhail's human fingerprints. Shifting back was not in the cards. Besides, he had gone limp in my arms again.

I took Troy's hand and relayed the message of waiting until the patrol passed. We had been in this spot for almost a full ten minutes between his run to see where we were and now, so there had to be a leviathan in the vicinity. And with the mist, the bleach scent was not as pronounced.

I took the spray bottle and pushed Troy aside, spraying the entrance to the alley before I took a step back, pulling him along with me. I hoped like hell that was enough to deter a heftier sniff of this alley, especially considering the mist had turned to a steady drizzle.

It didn't take long before the ground trembled at approaching feet. Large feet. The kind that belonged to a Godzilla-sized reptilian monster. The beast slowed to a stop near the alley, took a sniff of the air and then immediately sneezed.

"Damn building," it muttered and marched off.

We waited until the trembling lessened and then I tapped Troy. He turned and I tapped Adam behind me before grabbing onto Troy's belt. Adam's hand gripped my belt and our little caravan started on the last leg of our deadly adventure.

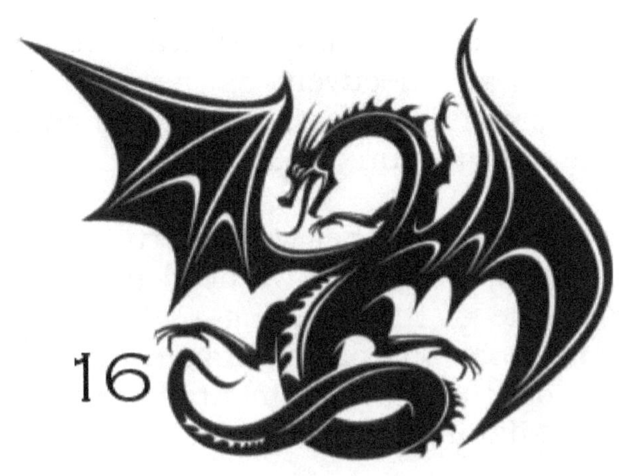

16

We kept close to the buildings as we slid down Pearl Street, in the direction of Fulton Street. When we passed the sign for John Street, I yanked on Troy's belt, trying to steer him across the street where the northwestern-most corner of Mikhail's apartment building stood.

Even in the near blackness surrounding us, I could make out the perceived destruction of the building, which was why I was sure Troy hesitated. Mikhail's building glamour still amazed me. All that ruse with silkscreens and decals, but it worked, and if we didn't want to get caught by the next patrol, we had to haul ass.

He glanced over his shoulder at me, and I nodded toward the building across the empty street and pushed him forward. He followed orders just as effectively as he issued them. Halfway across the street, the ground shook and we broke out in a run.

I had no idea whether we were running toward a leviathan or away, but we needed to get to the opposite side of the building so I could get us inside the lobby and out of danger. And now that we were on the move, I mentally repeated the sequence Mikhail had given me.

Three-five two-seven six-one. Three-five two-seven six-one. Over and over, with each step, the numbers flashed in my head. I prayed I'd get this right because I didn't think we'd get more than one shot at cracking the security system. If I entered it wrong, I feared the building would lock us out until Mikhail's hand could be scanned.

Of course, if that happened, we had better find another tight spot to hide. Otherwise, we would be easy pickings for the leviathans, especially if they swarmed. And if they all converged on us, we did not have enough bleach or firepower to take them down.

When we got close, I let go of Troy's belt and grabbed Adam's hand, pulling him into my place. I put on the speed, passing Troy. At the corner, I stopped and put my free hand up, stopping the procession. I glanced around the corner. Nothing moved in the darkness, and I exhaled, hoping that I wasn't missing anything in the direction of the door. The opposite way was just as clear, giving me the go-ahead to slip around the bend. The door was only a quarter of the way down the length of the building, and I ran my hand along the building's side next to the door, getting frustrated by the second, especially because that familiar tremor had started in the ground.

Somehow, I triggered the panel and the keypad appeared. I blinked at it and closed my eyes, inspecting my memory because I had totally blanked on the sequence during my search for the damn pad. I rubbed my fingers together and opened my eyes. Without overthinking it, I hit the numbers. Three, five, two, seven, six, and then the one. The panel closed and an almost imperceptible click sounded. I yanked the door open, and Troy held it, waving all of us inside the lobby.

He closed the door as quietly as he could and then stepped back, staring out at the street as the tremor turned to a rumble of feet. I sprayed the base of the door and backed up slowly, along with the rest of the men. This time, a group of young leviathans ran by the window without stopping. Like they smelled something that was worthy of attack. I glanced over my shoulder and mentally counted the group. There should have been seven of us. The caboose was missing.

My gaze met Troy's in the darkness and then a howl tore through the street. All our gazes swiveled toward the noise and then squeals followed. But the screaming did not stop, despite the painful wails of the leviathan. Troy stepped toward the door, and I grabbed his arm.

"Going out there now is suicide," I whispered. As if making my point, the pounding of adult leviathan feet shook the room and then at least a half-dozen pair of bone-crushing feet ran by.

We stood, helpless, as the human scream cut off.

I closed my eyes and took a breath. We had to put as much distance between us and the street level as possible. I crossed in the dark to the stairwell and opened the door, waiting until everyone was inside, including Troy. His pain was palpable on the air. But as soon as I shut the door on the lobby, drenching us in the complete blackness of an interior stairwell, I felt the wall for what I needed and hoped like hell Mikhail's grid was still operating and it extended through to the ground floor like it had throughout his apartment.

With the flip of a switch, the dull stairwell lights flicked on. Silence blanketed the small band of soldiers. Even with the death of one of their comrades, the presence of electricity made everyone's eyes widen. Troy blinked and then snapped his gaze to mine.

"Go," I whispered and pointed up the stairs. "I'll explain as soon as we put some distance between us and the ground floor."

Mikhail's eyes fluttered open. "Floor fifteen," Mikhail croaked from the crook of my arm. "Same code."

"You heard the dragon." I shooed them ahead and we climbed as silently as possible. I was certain Mikhail's penthouse was much higher than fifteen floors, but I wasn't going to argue with him in front of the troops. Not with having just lost another one of our own.

I would need to go searching through the building at some point to see what the floors held. Beyond the penthouse, I only was aware of the steel panic rooms that he had used to do my bidding. I still couldn't believe my stupidity. I nearly died from him blowing his flame at me.

Between the medical equipment he brought back to the penthouse, along with the fresh food, I was sure there was a meat freezer somewhere, along with a greenhouse. But what other surprises this building held would have to wait until we got to safety.

At floor fifteen stood another keypad. I hadn't noticed any others on the floors we passed, either. I stepped forward and pressed the same sequence in again. The door clicked and I pulled it open, waiting on the landing until everyone passed. As I stepped inside, I turned off the lights in the stairwell.

The first thing I noticed about this space: there were no windows. When I closed the stairwell door, it clicked again, locking us in the dark. I felt along the wall until I found another switch. A single bank of lights clicked on. It was enough to illuminate the entire open floor. A dozen cots lined one side, along with shelving that held clothing meant for a lab or a hospital. Towels and linens sat neatly folded next to the clothes. In the far-left corner stood an equally large double cabinet labeled First Aid. An industrial-style kitchen lined the other side, along with a half-dozen round cafeteria-style tables. The back wall had a men's restroom and women's restroom on either side. Immediately to our left before the line of cots, was a couple of industrial sized washers and dryers.

"What the hell?" Troy turned to me.

"My lab employees stayed here during highly focused testing," Mikhail said. "Showers are available and there should be enough frozen and dry goods to keep you until we can make that bomb. Just make sure you don't trash the place. If you use it, clean it."

Troy's head cocked like a puppy's would. "Showers?" His eyes lit up. I'm sure I looked the exact same way he did when I found out. "You have running water?"

"Yes. If you need me, use the call button." He nodded his head to the wall, where an intercom system sat.

"And where are you going?" Troy's eyebrows lowered into a suspicious glower.

"I need Woods to bring me to the medical ward."

Troy hooked his thumb toward the first-aid cabinets.

"I need more than what those cabinets hold," he said.

Troy glanced back at his team, who all were looking longingly at the rest rooms across the way. "Go clean up," he ordered. "I'm going with Woods and the dragon."

No one made any sort of stink at them being separated. In fact, they dropped all their equipment where they stood and made a beeline to the shelves, pilfering scrubs and towels before disappearing into the men's room.

"I just need Woods," Mikhail said.

"And I'm her superior, so either I'm taking you alone, or you can deal with both of us."

Mikhail grumbled but nodded, and I had to use the keypad to unlatch the door again. Troy stood over my shoulder, I'm sure to learn the code, but I typed it in too fast.

"What's the code?" he asked as the door closed behind us and I flicked the switch to illuminate the stairwell again.

I opened my mouth to tell him, but Mikhail interrupted. "Three-five-two-seven-six-one. Same as the building entry code."

He surprised me. I didn't think he'd give up his precious building codes so easily.

"Now that you have the code, you can run recovery patrols whenever you can without having Woods with you and your team."

Troy grunted and sent Mikhail a sideways glare.

"Would you prefer being my nursemaid while I heal?" Mikhail growled, his voice full of venom and anger.

I raised an eyebrow. "I'd actually prefer going on the mission," I mumbled.

"I'm not cut out for caretaking," Troy said, walking straight into the trap that Mikhail laid out for him. "I'll let Woods nurse you back to health, but you need to give me all the codes for all the rooms in this building. I don't want to be locked out, or locked in anywhere, understand?"

Mikhail glanced at me and then at Troy. "I'll give you access to everything except the penthouse. That is my domain and my domain only. As for the rest of the building, respect what you find, and don't fuck with the things in the lab. Understand?"

Troy's lips thinned. "Does she get the code to the penthouse?"

Mikhail exhaled through his nose and some smoke came with it. "No. It's my domain. No one gets that code."

We hit the landing for the twentieth floor and before I could berate him for his lack of trust, he interjected. "This is the floor. The code is three-five-one."

I punched in the numbers, and we entered. I did the same turn off the stairway lights, turn on the floor lights and turned, taking in the sterilization corridor we were in. The room beyond it held an operating table in the center and all the medical equipment that you would see in an operating room.

"When we get inside, I need you to put me on the table and then go clean up and get into sterilized scrubs because you will have to amputate my leg at the knee, and I would prefer not to get any more of an infection than I already have." He glanced at Troy. "You stay in here, please."

His voice carried such exhaustion, but I could not fathom doing what he was saying without help. "How?" I asked as the door whisked open.

"I can do it," Troy said. "I had field medical training overseas."

Mikhail glanced at him and nodded. "You both have to clean up, though."

Troy nodded, and I glanced at him and then Mikhail as we walked into the sterile room. I set him on the table and headed into the far room that had showers and sinks for sterilization before surgery and cleaning up after. My stomach knotted, but Troy was already stripping his clothing and heading toward the shower stall.

I didn't know where to look, but understood the need for expedience, especially because when I glanced through the window Mikhail was shifting back to human form and this time he cried out in pain. Thankfully, he kept his fire in check; otherwise, the entire medical suite would be compromised.

I stripped and stepped into the shower, taking the opposite spigot from Troy. I used the antibacterial soap on my entire form, including my hair, and then stepped out, taking a towel and drying off. I avoided eye contact with Troy as I dressed in the scrubs and the little paper shoes. Squeezing out the water from my hair, I curled it up into a messy bun and slipped a hair net over it. Before I walked into the surgical room, Troy handed me gloves and a mask.

"He did that to you?" he asked as he paused at the door.

I met his questioning gaze, knowing the burn scars on my back and legs were significant. "He did not want to, but I insisted it was the only way." I let out a laugh and looked through the window as the groans silenced. "In the end, he was right, and I should have listened to him and figured out a better story line." I shrugged and met Troy's gaze. "He nursed me back to health, so I have an obligation to do the same."

"Obligation," he huffed and opened the door, waving me inside without another comment.

Mikhail lay stretched out on the metal table, covered in sweat. He turned his head toward us and nodded toward the IV machine. "There are IV bags in the medical cabinet over there, along with a healthy supply of penicillin. I will need a bottle."

"That will kill you," Troy said.

Mikhail's lips tilted into a smile. "A dragon's metabolism burns through it much faster than a human's does. Besides, the infection is already hitting my bloodstream, so..."

I crossed to the cabinet and opened it. He wasn't kidding. There was an entire shelf of antibiotics, along with another full of morphine and other drugs all kept chilled in the refrigeration unit, including piles of IV bags and a few liters of blood. Mikhail was instructing Troy where the tools were and when I stepped back next to him, my face chilled at the array of things Troy had on a table next to the operating gurney.

My gaze locked on the bone saw and I swallowed hard.

Troy was in the process of cutting off Mikhail's pants.

"Woods," Mikhail snapped, pulling my attention to him.

I put the bottle on the table and hung the IV bag from the T-bar near Mikhail's head. He pointed at a needle in a plastic package. I picked it up.

"Give me that and the penicillin, and help me sit up."

I opened the package and handed him both items. I watched in fascination as he filled the entire length of the barrel with the contents of the bottle and then looked at me.

I stepped close and helped him sit up. Troy was smearing his right thigh and knee with iodine, and Mikhail took my hand and put it on his inner thigh.

"Find a vein for me," he said.

I glanced at his thigh, seeing exactly what was wrong. Too many red lines traversed from his knee.

"You don't want to hit the artery," Troy said. "That'll pump the medicine right out of him. You sure you don't want it in the arm?"

"Closer to the point of infection is better," Mikhail said.

Troy took the needle from him and ran his finger on the inside of Mikhail's knee, just above the damage. Next thing either of us knew, he plunged the needle in and slowly depressed the plunger until the plunge flange was flush with the barrel.

He then helped Mikhail lay back and took the IV and set it up in Mikhail's arm. "Grab me some of that morphine," he said as he set up a tourniquet around Mikhail's thigh.

"No," Mikhail said. "I don't want to be sedated, especially not with morphine. That shit will kill me."

Troy's eyebrows rose. "You really will need something."

Mikhail shook his head. "No. There's no time. Just cut it off before more poison gets into my bloodstream."

I went to take Mikhail's hand, but he shook his head.

"I'll crush it," he said and the flash of trepidation that crossed his eyes made me swallow hard. "Besides, he may need you to hand him things."

He took hold of the rails on the side of the table and looked at the ceiling. The sound of a bone saw yanked my gaze to Troy. He flipped his PPE over his face and focused on Mikhail's knee.

"Shouldn't you, like, use a scalpel or something first?" Heat enveloped me, and I recognized the panic seizing my muscles. But I was helpless to control it. Even deep breaths didn't help.

"There is no time. Tighten the tourniquet." Troy nodded to the strap around Mikhail's thigh. He didn't wait for me to follow through on the order. He just lowered the blade.

I scrambled to tighten the strap and I held it in place with all my strength. The belt dug into Mikhail's skin, leaving the area below an almost purple color. My stomach wanted to purge itself, but I swallowed back the bile. Maybe later I would let myself vomit, but for now, I needed to do everything Troy told me to so Mikhail wouldn't bleed out.

Mikhail stared at the ceiling without so much as a wince as the saw dug into the skin just below his knee. His forehead broke out into a sweat and the IV bag lowered faster than just a slow drip.

Blood splattered over both Troy and me as he cut through Mikhail's flesh.

But Mikhail didn't react until Troy hit bone. A low groan escaped through his tight lips, and he squeezed his eyes shut. His hands gripped the bars tight enough for the metal to creak from his hold.

A few moments later, Troy finished the dismembering of Mikhail's crushed appendage from the rest of his leg. He swept it away and grabbed clamps from his utility table and took the arteries in Mikhail's leg, clamping them shut before he quickly sutured them. He repeated the process with the veins as well until it seemed like the flow of blood slowed to a trickle.

"Let up on the pressure," Troy ordered.

I eased up as Troy stared at the oozing open stump. I had no idea what he was looking for, but when he held his hand up, I stopped loosening the tourniquet. He removed the clamps and then waited a moment; then he gave me a nod. I continued loosening the belt until there was no more pressure holding back Mikhail's blood. The stitches Troy had done held.

He picked up another tool that looked like a saw, but he held the flat end on the bones and turned it on, grinding the edges of Mikhail's tibia until it was smooth and flush with the muscle. He took bone cutters and extracted the small amount of the fibula that was left; then, he took the flap of skin he had left on the back of Mikhail's leg and pulled it over the amputated end and started stitching Mikhail back together.

It wasn't quite as much of a hack job as I had expected. I had a new respect for Troy's abilities despite his disgusted scowl that persisted throughout the surgery. I wasn't sure whether it was just doing the operation that painted that expression on his face or something deeper and darker.

But as he finished and stepped back, his gaze met mine and that scowl became unreadable.

17

Troy and I leaned against the wall in clean scrubs, sipping on bottled water we found in one of the cabinets, waiting for Mikhail to regain consciousness. He passed out at some point while Troy was mending his stump.

When he was finished with Mikhail, neither of us could leave the room in such disarray. It wasn't sanitary. We scrubbed the floor and the table, gathering all the waste, including Mikhail's leg, and bagged it up, along with all the bloody gauze pads and rags.

We even stripped Mikhail, cleaned him up, and put a johnny on him so he wouldn't freeze before we each took turns washing ourselves of all the mess in the shower.

With clean scrubs on, we checked on Mikhail again, but he remained unconscious. At least his breathing was regular, and he was not nearly as pale as he was when we came in. Even the lines in his leg had faded. Even so, Troy gave him another dose of penicillin just to be sure any chance of infection was knocked out of him. Then he replaced the intravenous bag and sauntered over to the other side of the room and took a seat on the floor, looking every bit as tired as I felt.

I crossed and took a seat next to him and let the last few hours sink in. The shakes started, but at least my stomach gave me a reprieve. I didn't throw up and I kept my hands clasped around my knees so Troy wouldn't see me shaking.

"Your surgery skills are impressive," I said when I felt my voice would not hold the tremors still accosting me. He had done an amazing job without so much as a flinch.

"The fact you didn't hurl or pass out impressed me." He glanced at me and then at the pristine room.

"I almost did," I admitted, and heat rose in my cheeks. I reached for my water, and he intercepted my hand.

"Look, even though you turned twelve different shades of green, you kept it down. Most wouldn't have been able to do that."

I stared at his hand holding mine, digesting his words and the way he gripped me. It wasn't gentle, and nowhere in the same vicinity as holding Mikhail's hand, but it still warmed me in a way I wasn't sure I liked. I glanced up at him.

"You're a good leader." I didn't know what else to say as I pulled my hand out of his grip and picked up the water. Uncapping the bottle and taking a sip gave me the precious seconds to figure out what else to say to the sudden awkwardness that crawled between us.

"I should check on the guys." He stood and glanced at Mikhail and then the floor before he looked at me. "He's it for you?" He hooked his thumb toward Mikhail.

I blinked at his blatant question and looked at the table where Mikhail's chest rose and fell in an even rhythm. When I met Troy's questioning gaze, he let out a small laugh and shook his head as his expression morphed from the cocked eyebrow to a scowl. Without another word, he headed toward the door. I remained seated, watching him go.

That little voice inside me said to stop him because I thought he had just opened a door that I hadn't even considered. And as flattered as I was, my heart belonged to the dragon on the table, even though that future was as doomed as we were.

I had a moment to wonder whether I would regret my silent inaction. But then the door to the operating room closed. The sound echoed in the sterile room like a tomb shutting forever.

"Should have stopped him." Mikhail's hoarse voice broke through the ringing in my ears.

I got to my feet and crossed to him as a hot flush of aggravation scraped my sterilized skin. *Why the hell was he pushing me away?* "Why?"

"I'm broken," he said, as if his physical state mattered to me at all. "He isn't."

I cocked my head and stared at him. That wasn't a valid reason to suggest I start something with someone else. "We all are broken, Mikhail." I sighed. "If you haven't figured that out yet, you're not as smart as I gave you credit for."

His lips cocked into a partial smile. "You aren't."

His comment pulled a laugh from my chest. He had no idea who I was if he didn't think I was marked by this war. In some ways, I was far more broken than he could ever be. "I'm just as broken as you are, so don't kid yourself." I handed him my water bottle. "What makes you think Troy is even interested, anyway?"

Mikhail took it without reservation and propped himself up with his left arm that wasn't hooked up to the intravenous liquid. He drained the bottle and then wiped his mouth with the back of his hand. "Thanks." He handed me the empty before lying back down on the steel table. "I've caught him glancing at you a couple times."

"So?"

"He's human. I'm not. I just thought it might be..." Mikhail trailed off and looked away as his eyes blazed in a way I'd never seen before. They flared almost green. "I need my bed." He blinked away the flames in his irises.

"Did I just detect... jealousy?" I asked, amused by his reaction.

"No. I just need some rest. And I need you to help me to my bed in the penthouse." He avoided my gaze.

"And how do you suggest we get you there?"

"It's only ten more flights." He methodically removed the lines from his arm and handed them to me, busying himself with anything that seemed to keep him from meeting my gaze. "You can dump all the trash in the incinerator over there." He pointed to a metal door in the opposite wall. "It fires up when it's full."

"Ah." I couldn't think of anything witty to say to him. Not with the conflict written in his body language. It was as if truly admitting he felt something other than being my caretaker wasn't in his makeup. I took the line and the empty bag off the T-bar and crossed, opened the metal chute and dumped the line and bag, because I needed the time for my own self-reflection.

Troy was a handsome man, but with the interest he showed today, there seemed to be an underlying hostility and I really didn't want to try to crack that nut. Not when my heart belonged to the damn dragon, despite how much that made me feel like a traitor to my own kind.

I dumped the garbage bag that we had packed with all the rags and leftovers from surgery down the incinerator path as well and then finally turned my attention back to Mikhail. But he was no longer in human form. I had been too deep in thought to hear his transition.

A little one-legged dragon met my gaze.

"Bring a couple doses of penicillin and a couple of needles." He gruffly barked the order, as if he were just as annoyed with me as I was with him.

His tone crawled across my skin, and I tightened my jaw, grinding my teeth.

Why couldn't we both just be honest with each other for a second?

I turned and grabbed a plastic box off the shelf and put two bottles of antibiotics and needles into the container, along with a tube of topical antibiotics and a couple sets of bandages. His leg dressings would need to be changed whether he was in dragon form or human form, and I didn't want to be running up and down ten flights of stairs multiple times a day.

"Can you also grab one of those containers of green gel?" He pointed to the lower shelf that had four canisters of what he asked for.

I had no clue what it was, but maybe it was some antibiotic gel that could be spread on his leg easier than the paste-like topical ointment. "Anything else?"

"As many towels as you can grab. A scalpel, a needle, and some suture string," he added to my growing list.

I stared at him as the items sunk into my tired brain. "What the hell do we need a scalpel for?"

"If I have a prayer of ever walking again, I need you to put that green gel directly on the break in my spine."

What did he just say? "What the fuck? Why didn't you have Troy do that while he was here?"

If a dragon could press his lips into an invisible line, that's what Mikhail's expression was, but he finally opened his mouth after a few heartbeats. "Because that's dragon blood and it is very rare. I didn't want him to know it existed and that it has healing properties that seem miraculous." He met my gaze. "Besides, once you do what I ask, I cannot move until it does its thing, and the only place I'll be in a comfortable position is on my bed."

"I've seen you bleed, and it doesn't look like this." I shook the container.

"That's because I'm not a full-blooded dragon. I'm a half-breed. Remember?" Even his tone challenged me, like anything I said would be the wrong thing.

My brain just caught up to what he said about the contents. "Miraculous how? And exactly how long do you have to remain still?"

"It has healing properties. And as far as how long I'll be laid up, it could be hours or days. It depends on how damaged my back is. If the nerve is severed, I'm not sure it will work, but if it is just pinched or even nicked, I have a chance."

Healing properties. "Could you have used this on my back?"

"No. Not without risking your life further." He met my gaze. "I thought of it, but sometimes humans have a deadly reaction to it and I did not want to take that chance."

"Oh." Right, because if he had and it killed me, he never would have known my secret about bleach. I looked at the green goop and then put the container in the box. Before I closed it, I added a second canister of dragon blood just in case, and then dumped the items he listed off in and snapped the lid, turning back toward the diminutive dragon lying prone on the table.

I studied him. He was such the opposite of that big bad dragon that I encountered in Grand Central, and it had nothing to do with his injuries. That fire in his gaze had dulled and he seemed... softer. Less menacing.

I wondered whether it was just the exhaustion playing tricks on me. "Before I do any sort of surgery on you, I need a nap."

His stare hardened. "It has to be as soon as we step inside. I've gone longer than I should have and if we wait, there will be no chance of recovery."

Great. Now his entire future was in my lap.

"What if I screw up because I'm so tired? What if I sever your spinal cord trying to open you up?" I snarled as I stalked toward him.

"We will deal with it if that happens." His eyes closed. "Look, Holly, I need you to carry me upstairs and then cover the bed with those towels and put me on them. I'll shift and then I'll direct you as to what to do. I trust you." His eyes opened to that shimmering citrine that I had gotten used to.

"Fine." I dropped the container into a bag with a dozen towels and hauled it over my shoulder before I picked him up in my arms. "I swear, you just like to nuzzle up to my breast," I muttered as we crossed and stepped out through the sterilizing air lock.

He let out a soft chuckle. "Would that really be so bad?"

I rolled my eyes and started the ten-story trek with Mikhail nestled against me.

18

Ten floors with legs that already felt like spaghetti was not a picnic, especially carrying Mikhail and the bag of medical supplies, along with a load of towels slung over my shoulder. By the time I got to the landing for the penthouse, I was out of breath, and I had to put the package down before I focused on the keypad because he obviously didn't have keys on him this time.

"Two, four, six, eight, zero, five, pound, star," Mikhail said.

I glanced at him. "Any significance?" I asked as I typed the simple passcode.

"None. Just easy to remember," he said as I swung the door open to a sun-drenched apartment and shuffled the bag inside with my foot before we followed. No wonder I was so tired. His leg surgery and the cleanup took all night. The last time I had slept was at least twenty-four hours ago, when we had the entire crew with us. Now we were down by four, with a severely injured dragon.

I shook the exhaustion away and punched the code in again, reengaging the lock. "And you really thought I wouldn't have been able to figure that out?"

The little dragon grinned, and I had to stop the urge to just drop him and let him fend for himself. Only this being could swing my moods as wide as a pendulum.

"You would have put way too much thought into it," he answered.

I snorted a laugh at his comment, swinging the emotions back to humor. He was right; I would never have guessed as easy a combination as what he had for this place. "And the front door. What significance is that code?"

"That was mine and my wife's and kids' birthdays."

His answer silenced me.

I had guessed that might be the representation, but I hadn't been sure. *He did have some sentimental bones in his body.*

Although we may have just removed the only one left. The last thought nearly sent me into another fit of laughter. I was way too tired to do surgery on Mikhail. *What the hell was he thinking?*

"When's your birthday?" I asked, trying to focus my mind on something other than what he had asked of me.

"June first."

Even as my mind wandered to spring and started making plans for a birthday that I had no idea whether either of us would reach, I crossed into the bedroom and set him down on the chair. Once the bed was covered in the multiple layers of towels, I hoped it was enough. If not, his mattress would be ruined. My brain kept swirling, kept trying to avoid the inevitable, and I turned, moving him from the chair and onto my towel mound. I placed him gently on his stomach and stepped back.

Transforming from dragon to human was slower this time, unlike that first time in Grand Central where it was within a blink. And it wasn't nearly as fast as his shift in the tunnels either. Maybe that was a true indication of just how broken he really was. When he finished, a sheen of sweat glistened on his bare back.

The johnny he wore lay open, giving me a full view of his perfectly shaped ass and thighs. The bandages on the stump of his leg were soaked through and would need changing as well. I pulled the chair close to the bed as he turned his face toward me.

"Can you get a damp cloth from the bathroom and wipe off my back?" His tired eyes met mine like dull mirrors into his pain.

The soft question was not in any way demanding and I gave him a smile. "Sure." I got a hand towel out of the cabinet and wet it, making sure it wasn't too cold. When I came back into the bedroom, I took a seat on the edge of the bed and gently ran the towel over his backside, cleaning him off before I reached for the bandages on his leg.

"That can wait until after," he said.

I swallowed and nodded as fear coiled like lead in my belly. "You'll have to talk me through this," I said, silently wishing that Troy was here to do the surgery part. The idea of slicing Mikhail's skin made my stomach tighten in the most uncomfortable way. But I had to just suck it up.

He grabbed his pillow and hugged it with his face toward me. "The break is in the lumbar area. My upper thighs and hips feel like pins and needles, but from the middle of my thigh down, I feel nothing."

I looked at his lower back, specifically at the bruise above his fine ass. "You have a bruise."

"Can you run your finger down my spine and see if you can feel the damage? Start in the middle of my back and don't stop until you feel the normal spine again, okay?"

I did as he suggested, running my fingers down, feeling each disc and the strong cords of muscles on either side. When I got to the top of the bruise, it changed under my fingers, bulging out in a weird jut. His breath sucked in for a moment. Below the jut, his spine seemed to disappear for about an inch before the natural bumps like the spine above the bruise resurfaced.

"I know where the damage is," I said. "It's about two inches in total right after the start of the bruise."

"You're going to need to cut a little above and end a little below that area."

"I really don't know if I can do this," I said staring at my shaking hands. "I could go get Troy."

Mikhail closed his eyes. "You are the strongest woman I have ever met. I need *you* to do this, now. Besides, I do not trust Troy. And waiting for you to run down the stairs and back is not an option."

"Damn it, Mikhail, what if I fuck up?"

He met my gaze. "Then I remain paralyzed."

I sucked in a loud inhale and searched his eyes. His cross expression softened and his brow smoothed out as he seemed to push down whatever aggravation had bled into his voice.

"Holly, you have the opportunity to possibly fix that. It's no guarantee, but every second you waffle is a step toward this being permanent," he said with a softness to his voice that belied the urgency in his eyes.

"Shit. Way to put the pressure on." As much as I did not want to do this, his argument was compelling enough for me to at least attempt this insanity. "Are you sure I'm the one with a death wish?"

His half tilt of a grin and shoulder shrug made me want to slap his ass good and hard, but I refrained. Instead, I set the medical supplies out on the towel next to him and picked up the scalpel.

"Where do I cut?" I asked before I chickened out.

"Right over the spine. Just give me a minute." He pushed the pillow away and set his forehead down on his folded arms so I couldn't see his face. But the muscles in his jaw tightened. "You'll need to do a T cross at the top and bottom after you do the initial incision and then peel back the skin so you can see the bone underneath. Once you do that, you'll have to spread the contents of one of the jars down the length of the bone that's visible.

From the good section, through the bad and back to the good. Then you can close the skin and stitch it up."

"Why didn't we do this with your leg?" The question bubbled up from my need to stall. His directions haunted me, and I couldn't fathom why, if this dragon blood was such a healing elixir, he didn't take this route with his crushed leg.

"My leg was crushed beyond repair, my back..." He sighed and glanced at me. "I still have a chance as slight as it is, it's still worth the attempt."

I nodded, took a breath to settle all the doubts building in my mind, and steadied my hand with the scalpel to the spot just over the bruise and then recentered it a few centimeters higher. "Tell me when you're ready."

A few deep breaths and then I saw the muscles actually relax throughout his back. It was as if someone gave him a strong sedative.

"Go," he said.

I lowered the scalpel and paused right before I touched his skin. I couldn't go through the spine and cause more damage, but I had to go deep enough to actually reach the bone. I almost chickened out, but his words propelled me forward. This was an attempt to fix what may have already been done. If I didn't try, he definitely wouldn't walk again. He might never fly again, either, from what he had said, and we needed him to fly in order to deliver the bleach bomb we had yet to build.

I let my mind mull over things, but my hand sliced through skin until the blade hit bone, and then I dragged it lower at the same depth, over and through the area that was damaged. Mikhail groaned, but did not move. I finished the first cut and then did a couple of T cuts at the top and bottom of my incision.

Blood seeped down his sides as I peeled back the skin, and I ignored the flip of my stomach at the clear view of his mangled spine. I wasn't sure this would work, but I quickly took the cap off the green goop and spread the dragon blood over the visible damage, doing exactly as directed. One jar was more than enough, and I used every last ounce of that thick blood before I folded the skin back together. I dried my hands with the hand towel before I took the silk and threaded the suture needle.

I took my time trying to stitch him up as neatly as I could, but I was not as skilled with sutures as Troy. When I finished, I spread antibiotic ointment over the crude capital "I" carved in his back and covered it with gauze.

I got a clean towel and wiped up his sides before I went into the bathroom and dumped the soiled cloth into the hamper. When I finished cleaning off his blood from my arms and from under my nails, I turned and fell on my knees before the toilet, vomiting a hot stream of bile that had coated my throat through most of the hack job I did on his back.

With a shaky hand, I flushed the toilet, and then crossed to the sink and splashed cold water over my face and brushed the vile taste from my mouth. I couldn't wipe out the dirty feeling and stripped out of the soiled scrubs. The shower felt heavenly and the need to feel clean ebbed away with the sweet scent of soap that filled the steam. I closed my eyes, letting the water wash the stress from my body. When I finished, my fingers had pruned up and I dried off before combing out the knots from my hair.

I had no idea how long I had been in the shower, but I needed it as badly as Mikhail needed me to cut his back open. Without a stitch of clothing on, I crossed to the closet and perused his wife's clothing until I found a similar dress to the crushed velvet one Mikhail had insisted I bring with us last time.

This was cotton with short sleeves, but it was just as comfortable on my tired skin as that crushed velvet had been. A part of me wished I still had that with me, despite it being soiled with my own blood.

I turned and Mikhail stared at me with a cocked eyebrow. The glow from his eyes was duller than usual.

"I needed something clean," I explained and smoothed the dress.

He pulled the pillow back under his head with a nod, and his eyes closed. "I think I might need another dose of penicillin," he said with a slurred voice. He straightened his arm out to the side.

I didn't hesitate and without direction, I filled the canister of the needle with the entire contents of the drug vial, plucked the needle with my finger to get any air bubbles out, and then turned his arm. His veins already stood out against his skin, and I slid the needle into one and depressed the plunger, sending medicine he needed into him.

"Thank you," he whispered after I took the needle out. He pulled his arm back under the pillow.

"Is there anything else I can get you?"

"No. You can lay down and get some sleep, though. You look like you need it." He looked at me with one eye and then that fluttered closed.

I didn't think I'd be able to sleep. Not after the last two surgeries I participated in. But the exhaustion pounding in my temple said otherwise. I crawled onto the far side of the bed, pushing the edges of the soiled towels closer to Mikhail and stretched out, facing him.

I studied his profile and then let my gaze drift over his strong arms and his upper back. I glanced back at his face before I got to the patch job I did, and his citrine eyes studied me with open adoration.

"Don't look at me like that," I said even though I could live the rest of my life under the light of that stare. It warmed my soul the way no other ever had.

"Like what?"

"Like I am special to you." I rolled onto my back and chose to stare at the ceiling as silence pervaded the room.

"You are."

I turned my gaze to him. "It's just transference." I repeated what he had spouted to me in that concrete garage we found ourselves in after leaving this place to make our way back to my platoon. That had only been days ago, yet it felt like weeks.

"No, Holly. It's a little deeper than that," he said, jarring me.

He chose now to declare his feelings? Now, when all I can see is his blood spilling on the floor? I backed right into denial. "No, Mik. It's not." I returned my gaze to the ceiling. "It is impossible."

He let out a huff of a laugh. "Apparently nothing is impossible with you."

"You are a sappy fuck when you're injured." I glanced back at him and damn him, he flashed that endearing smile that made my knees weak. Thankfully, I was already lying down.

His smile faded as his eyes fluttered closed. A heavy sigh followed and then the cadence of his breathing when sleep gripped him filled the room.

I turned my gaze back to the ceiling, wondering yet again how the hell I was going to get my heart out of his grip. He was a dragon, after all, and as much as I was enthralled by him right now, it would never work. Especially if we failed at our attempt to stop this war.

19

Sleep yanked me deep into the abyss and with it came nightmares.

Nightmares of leviathans shredding Mikhail to pieces while the Serpent King laughed, and I watched, unable to save him.

A hand touched my face, and I jerked with a gasp. Troy's blue eyes stared at me from the spot where Mikhail should have been. "You've been sleeping for two days," he said.

I blinked and sat up.

My gaze took in the darkened bedroom. When I looked back at the figure next to me, Mikhail was there and snoring in that light way of his that sounded like a chair scraping in the distance. I reached over, but it seemed like the distance was impossibly far. Stretching even more than humanly possible, my fingers finally grazed the edge of the bandage. I pulled it back away from Mikhail's skin but there was no ugly incision on his back, just a bulge in his spine that seemed to be pulsing. I quickly covered it up again, confused.

I had done what he asked, hadn't I? Doubt as thick as the low-lying fog that rolled through the room scratched at my mind.

He turned toward me. "My lower right leg has been hurting for hours." His voice was groggy and off. Like it wasn't Mikhail speaking. It actually reminded me of the Serpent King's awful voice, and I shivered.

"You don't have anything below your right knee anymore." When I glanced at his leg, it was shredded to bits, with strings of flesh hanging from his knee; bits of bone scattered on the towels and blood poured from his stump. Much more blood than I had ever seen. It soaked the bed, spreading toward me like the breaching of a flood plain. I pulled my legs up higher, away from the advancing mess, and my chest hurt with the thunder of my heart.

I dumped the container of dragon blood in a line around me, hoping it would stop the blood from reaching me like bleach stops leviathans. When Mikhail's blood hit the green line, it burst into flame, driving me off the bed and sending me running to find help.

"Dragons run hot," Mikhail called from the bedroom and then broke out in a laugh that nearly scared the piss out of me. But then he added, "When you come back, bring a set of crutches."

The stairway elongated as his laughter followed me down. It seemed to take forever to get to the floor that the soldiers were on. I stared at the keypad and blinked.

The outside street surrounded me, and I held a dragon egg. Jenny stood beside me, but half her body was blackened from the blast. "Beware of Troy. He has ulterior motives."

When I turned to face her, something yanked her into the shadows. I turned back to the door, trying to keep the egg nestled in my arm. But Troy was there, with a mouthful of sharp teeth like a shark.

He swung his fist down, smashing the dragon egg in my arms. My stomach dropped, and I turned away to be standing in the soldier's room with a biting need to have Troy come tend to Mikhail.

Troy sat at one of the tables with a coffee, with everything perfectly in place and a smile that made me pause. His teeth were normal, and he had never truly smiled at me. More like glowered, but here he was beaming.

Suspicion flowed through my blood like hot syrup as I crossed to the table. My bare feet padded across the cool industrial floor. Each step sent a jolt through my bones until I stood opposite Troy. "I need you to look at Mik. I don't think he's okay."

Of course he wasn't. Fire probably had taken him and everything else in the apartment. My heart jumped and the urgency increased.

Troy's eyes sharpened. "So, you're going to let me into his private quarters?" he asked with a smile toying on his lips like it was something taboo.

Everything about Troy seemed taboo at this point and Jenny's strange warning surfaced, but I rolled my eyes at him.

I did not have time for this. We needed to get back to Mikhail. "We need to stop on twenty so I can grab crutches for Mikhail." This seemed to be more important right now than checking on Mikhail, and I couldn't fathom why.

A strange need pulled me right into the operating room and I turned, blinking at the surroundings. The walls and floor were painted with blood, except it wasn't red; it was green. I gasped as red blood pooled on the operating table. If it fell, the room would burst into flame.

I spun around, and Troy stared down at me. "I find myself very bothered by the idea of you and the dragon... together." His piercing blue eyes stared down at me as if I were his prey.

My heart sped up. What was between Mikhail and me was none of his business. I went to speak, to tell him just that, but he advanced with a feral hunger written on his face, pulling his lips into a knowing smile. His eyes carried such intensity that I swallowed hard.

"What if we are the last ones alive?" he asked as he cornered me.

I cocked my head, as my mouth dried up. My glance went to the operating table and the red blood slowly creeping toward the sides.

"The only humans left on Earth?" he clarified

His question crawled under my skin like a tick, festering, separating the need to get out to include the need to look at Troy. He kept my gaze, but there was something underneath all these questions and it went back to his first statement.

"Is this all about humanity or is this about you?" I narrowed my gaze at him. "Are you jealous of Mikhail?"

"I'm human. He's not."

Weren't those the same words Mikhail had used last night?

He started to turn away and I went to grab his arm. He moved like lightning, grabbing my wrist and slamming me against the wall. His chest rose and fell like he was trying to control a wild beast inside him. Instead of answering me, he crushed his lips down on mine.

My mouth popped open in surprise, and he took the opportunity to explore my mouth with his tongue. The low groan that came from the back of his throat both chilled me and sent a thrill through my entire form. I had not been with anyone for a very long time, and Troy knew what he was doing.

I found myself sinking into the kiss, my heart pounding hard enough to remind me of how alive I was. My free hand pressed against his chest, feeling the same heightened pulse from him. His hand descended my arm, finding my breast, and his soft caress belied the demanding kiss.

God, I needed this. But what would Mikhail do if he found out?

God knows my body was screaming at me to ravage him, but the blood on the table had just breached the edge. We had to move or we would die in here. I pushed Troy's chest, moving him away. "Mikhail will kill you."

The way he grinned sent chills through me, and a panicked sweat broke out on the back of my neck. It was as if he didn't want to leave this room. It was as if he wanted us to go up in flames.

"Not if I kill him first," he said and was gone.

My heart thundered and I grabbed the crutches. The route to the stairwell elongated like one of those funhouse mirrors, and my sprint became sluggish, like I couldn't stop the inevitable. I burst through the door to the stairs just as the operating room flashed into hot flames.

The next door I flew through was the one for the penthouse. Troy's gait through the living room slowed, as if I had never lost sight of him.

He spun around and glared at me. "I guess money does buy everything," he snarled at me. "Including your alliance." He turned and looked down at the street below and his shoulders tensed.

I was not in the mood for his anger or the accusations flashing over his face. "Stop acting like a damn teenager."

As I stood next to him at the window, the world below changed into a landscape of writhing leviathans crawling onto the shore. Thousands of them poured onto the street like ants fleeing a drowning ant hill. My skin seemed to shrink, pulling me into myself.

He glanced sideways at me. "Those things are multiplying by the minute."

"Your point?"

He looked at the leviathans below, his anger bleeding away and his expression growing serious. "Can he do what he says he can?" he asked without looking at me. Doubt pervaded his tone.

"Yes. It doesn't matter if he can walk or not; his mind is still sharp. Just look at this building. He's made it functional on its own grid and disguised it to the outside world. Both human and monster from the street level think this is one of the destroyed buildings. If he can do that, a bomb ought to be a snap." I had faith in Mikhail's abilities.

I turned toward the bedroom. "Time to check his leg."

He grabbed my hand and pulled me into his arms. "I want a chance."

"A chance for what?" I asked, but I already knew, and it really was hopeless. As hopeless as Mikhail and I having any future. But if I was putting my bets on one of them, it was the one who had already captured my heart whether I liked it or not.

"A chance for you to see someone other than a dragon." He glanced toward the bedroom and then met my gaze. "Please."

Fuck. I knew his intentions. I knew he wanted a physical relationship with me, which was more interest than Mikhail had shown. Hell, I needed to scratch my own itch in a very bad way. I hated this precarious position. Plus, his question had burrowed under my skin as well.

What if we were all that was left of the human race?

That meant I was the only one able to carry children and perpetuate the species. Double fuck.

And he said please. Triple fuck.

I was in one hell of a corner with only one way out. I nodded and a growl from the bedroom made us both turn.

Mikhail stood on one leg, hugging the doorjamb with the johnny skewed off one shoulder. He had such an angry glare that I attempted to pull my hand from Troy's grip, but it was impossible.

My heart thundered. "You shouldn't be up."

He huffed, like it didn't matter. "I'll be fine," he growled.

I finally yanked my hand free and started across the room. He put his hand up and shook his head, as if I had somehow betrayed him.

"Go." He pointed at the door.

"The fuck I am," I snarled back, suddenly more furious than I had been in a very long time. "What is it with you?" I yelled. "Thinking I'm a fucking possession of yours. You don't own me. So, this crap stops now." I pointed at Mikhail. "You and I have some shit to work through before you have the right to give me any rage on whatever choices I make."

I stomped into Mikhail's office and slammed the door. The walls shook with the force. I didn't want to deal with the emotional and physical pull between dragon and human right now. Not when we had armies marching up from the deep in numbers that scared the shit out of me.

I turned, and Mikhail stood inside the door on both legs, like he had so many weeks ago when I had found solace in the library. I hadn't even heard the door open.

He crossed the distance gracefully, as though he had never been injured. "I'm in love with you."

His simple statement nearly took me out at the knees. "Then why the fuck did you tell me I should have gone after him last night? Why the mixed signals?"

"He's human and not broken like I am."

"We are all fucking broken!"

He grabbed my face and kissed me so gently that it silenced me. "I'm sorry," he whispered after his lips left mine. "I was not thinking clearly, and obviously my pushing you toward Harrington wasn't well thought out." He took a deep breath and met my gaze.

"Mikhail," I said softly, pressing my cheek into his palm.

"He wants to fuck you. But I want a life with you. I don't care if it's a day or a thousand years, either."

"I need sex," I blurted and my cheeks immediately heated. I couldn't see being with someone without consummating the relationship in any way.

Mikhail chuckled. "I am a man. I probably need it more than you do."

I blinked at him. "But you never showed any real interest in me."

He rubbed his thumb across my cheek. "You were injured and the one time you got all uppity about it had been after I collected my family's heads. I wasn't anywhere near the right frame of mind after that ordeal. But that wasn't because you are not desirable." His eyes moved from mine, down the front of my dress and back. "I am not so different from Troy in my wants either, but I know there is a time and place for intimacy, and we have not been given the chance for that yet."

Holy fuck. I stared at him, melting from his words. Instead of speaking, I pulled him to my lips and this time the kiss was not a chaste brushing. This time, I demanded more. Oh, and he delivered in spades.

Mikhail St. Clare knew how to kiss. His tongue gently explored my mouth and he pulled me into his arms, deepening the experience. His gentle expertise slipped to more aggressive, as if he just gave in to all his feelings. It was magical, until he pulled away.

He stared into my eyes. "I need to know how you feel," he said with a raspy voice filled with the same need coursing through my veins.

"There are times I hate you, like when you haul me over your shoulder as if I'm a useless human."

His lips twitched into a smile. "And other times?"

"Other times I could just throttle you for being so damn blind."

His smile faded. "I was not blind. I was in denial. Because, seriously, how could you love me after all that I've done to your kind?"

I blinked at his words. They seemed more like my thoughts than anything that would come from Mikhail. "I care a great deal, but I need to get laid so I can think straight again."

He snorted laughter. "I stopped fucking for fuck's sake a long time ago."

"Maybe you should start again."

"Maybe I will, but the bed is a god-awful mess. And you, my dear, are ovulating, so today is not the day for fucking."

I balked and he pushed me back in the seat.

"But that doesn't mean I can't give you a preview of what life with me would mean for you."

He tore my dress in half, straight up the middle, with no effort at all. I gasped as he pushed my legs apart and lowered his mouth to my core.

 20

Shaking. Someone was shaking me. My eyes flew open to the darkness of the bedroom. Mikhail trying to shake me awake.

"Holly. I need more penicillin," he said with a groggy voice.

I blinked at the blackness surrounding us and then at the vividness of what felt like moments ago. Jesus, it must have been a dream. "What time is it?" I reached for the light on the nightstand and flipped it on.

"I don't know."

I turned back to him and gasped. He was bathed in sweat and both bandages had been soaked through. And not by perspiration. His eyes were bloodshot, and he was as pale as I'd ever seen him. My strange dream evaporated.

Fear enveloped me. Mikhail needed help.

"Oh, fuck," I whispered. My hands shook as I opened the container that held the last dose of medicine and the needle. I stripped the sterile packaging off the needle and unscrewed the medicine, stuck it inside and pulled the contents into the canister. I tapped the needle to get out any air and then took a slow and steadying breath.

"Easy," he whispered and held out his arm.

I closed my eyes and breathed a few more times to shake my complete disorientation out of my head. "When I'm done, I need to go get Troy." My voice cracked.

He didn't argue. He just watched me with a perplexing gaze. After I finished, he said, "Thank you."

"I need to go get Troy, okay?"

He nodded. "You talk in your sleep."

Beyond the pain, I saw some humor in his eyes.

My heart hammered and I wasn't sure whether it was because of his state or what he may or may not have heard. It was becoming more and more fuzzy to me by the minute. He just smiled in a way that made me shift.

"We can talk about it when I'm not in such a sorry state," he said. "I need soldier boy to make sure..." He looked away like he didn't want to say the words. "To make sure I'm not dying." His eyes found mine.

My heart jumped in my throat, and I bolted. My hand still shook as I punched in the code. I barely remembered the stairwell light and then I was running down the stairs at a pace that if I tripped would kill me. But the way Mikhail said what he did set my heart on triple beat.

I punched in the code for the room on fifteen and raced in, throwing the light switch. My gaze flew over the cots until I zeroed in on Troy, ignoring the growling and grumbling to turn off the lights. I crossed and grabbed his hand, pulling him out of the cot and toward the door. I didn't care that he was only in a wifebeater and skivvies, either.

"Something's wrong," I said.

That seemed to wake him up in full. He swiped the lights off as we exited and took the stairs two by two, stopping at the twentieth floor. He started punching in the code and I grabbed his hand, pulling him up the stairs.

"He's in the penthouse," I said and without further explanation, we catapulted up the remaining ten flights. The door was still cracked from my run. I closed it and flipped on the lights, pointing toward the bedroom.

Troy gave me a cursory look and headed that way as I leaned back against the door, trying to catch my breath.

"Christ, what the hell did you do to his back?"

I stumbled into the bedroom. Troy held the bandage in his hand. The ugly I stood out against his back but now there were red lines coming from the sutured skin. He looked around, then headed into the bathroom and came out a few moments later with a bottle of peroxide. He poured it over the wound.

Mikhail hissed as his eyes popped open.

"Seriously, Woods, what the fuck did you do?" he asked again as he tossed the now empty bottle into the garbage.

"She did what I asked," Mikhail said.

"Well, whatever she did, your body is rejecting it."

"My left foot is tingling."

"The lines coming from her crude incision tell me whatever you had her do, it's poisoning you. You are burning up."

"Dragons run hot," both Mikhail and I said at the same time.

Troy sent me a glare. "Go get more antibiotics and some iodine from downstairs. Along with a clean scalpel. I'm going to try to fix this."

I stopped. "Your left leg?" I asked, turning back.

"I still can't move it to bang out the pins and needles."

"It's working then."

I just got a shoulder raise in response.

Troy pointed. "Please get me what I asked for so we can remove the infected skin." His voice was a little softer this time. "I'll look at his leg too, but I don't see any evidence of blood poisoning."

I nodded.

As I was leaving, he scolded Mikhail for having a rookie do a surgery like that. The admonishment was received with a grumbled apology from the patient.

I grabbed the bag that I had used to bring things upstairs last time and went down the ten floors to the medical unit. I filled the bag with both topical and intravenous antibiotics, needles and a scalpel, and grabbed a couple bottles of iodine, along with nearly all the bandages. On the bottom shelf next to the dragon blood was a vial, and I picked it up. I stared at one of the vials of morphine and added it to the mix along with an alternative, oxycodone, just in case whatever Troy was going to do to him was more painful. As I was walking out, I grabbed a pair of crutches on impulse.

I was out of breath when I got back to the apartment and this time, I engaged the keypad to lock up. The type of exhaustion that made my stomach do a slow roll gripped me as I crossed to the bedroom.

Mikhail's leg was wrapped in clean bandages and the old ones had been stuffed in the garbage. Troy extended his hand, and I put the iodine, scalpel, and painkillers in his hand along with a wrapped needle, careful not to stab him with the sharps.

"I didn't have nearly enough sleep." He wiped his face with his free hand. "Are there better lights in here?"

"There's a light stand in the library," Mikhail said, looking over at me.

His voice slurred in a way that concerned me.

I went and found the light, unplugging it and carrying it into the bedroom. I plugged it in and turned it on high right next to where Troy stood, careful not to blind him with the lights. It truly illuminated his back.

How could I have thought the dragon blood would be a miracle cure? Right now, it looked like a child carved him up, and my stomach tightened.

How could I have thought that dream was real?

I looked at the two central figures who had starred in my dream and wondered how I would really react if the same situations presented themselves. Would I shun Troy for Mikhail? Did the dragon truly own my heart? The only thing real about the dream was I indeed needed this horny itch scratched. But right now, all I wanted was for Mikhail to be okay.

"Morphine or oxycodone?" Troy asked.

"Oxy. I'm allergic to morphine," Mikhail said.

"Keep him entertained," Troy said to me and pointed to the spot next to his head. "This is not going to be pleasant." He sent me a grimace and only loaded the needle with a small dose of oxycodone and waited until I was seated with my back to the headboard before he shot it into Mikhail's ass.

Mikhail's brow furrowed, and I ran my hand through his hair like I had done on the stairs. He tilted his head so he could see me and put his hand out. I put mine in his without thinking and held on, even when he squeezed his eyes closed. He didn't squeeze any tighter, like he was still mindful of my frailty even in the midst of his agony.

I kept stroking his temple as worry ran through my bones like a contagion.

"I think we should talk about your dream." He opened his glossy eyes and winked at me, which made me second-guess grabbing the drugs.

Troy glanced up for a moment, and then back down as his jaw tightened. The nuance of aggravation flushed his features and then he shook it away and refocused on what he was doing.

"I dreamed they were multiplying in the thousands and flooding the streets." I swallowed. "And we were the last ones left on Earth."

"Sometimes I think we are," Troy said as he worked.

"There are more of you hiding in places they can't discern," Mikhail said. "As long as no one cuts themselves, they are safe."

My gaze snapped to his back. Human blood was one thing; dragon blood was another. Those beasts could home in on dragon blood from miles away. "Your blood," I whispered.

"Air is filtered." Mikhail met my gaze. "The only place it isn't is the lobby."

"So don't bleed in the lobby," Troy said with a nod, like he needed something else to concentrate on too.

"Boy picks up fast." Mikhail gave me a lopsided grin. "But that really wasn't what you were talking about in your sleep."

"How much oxy did you give him?" I asked Troy.

"Just enough to take the edge off while I do this," he said, still cutting away the inflamed and rotting flesh, along with scraping away as much pus as he could. He shook his head as he worked, silently moving his lips in what looked like a stream of swears. He poured more iodine over the wound and then looked up at me. "You don't still happen to have some of that liquid bandage, do you?"

"No. I think it's with the rest of our stuff down with the bleach."

"Do you have butterfly bandages?" he asked Mikhail.

"In the bathroom. Under the sink, behind the towels, there's all sorts of stuff," Mikhail muttered.

Troy pointed his chin toward the bathroom. I peeled my hand out of Mikhail's and went to look for whatever he had stowed away in the cabinet. He had quite a few first-aid kits and boxes of bandages of all sizes. Even one still in a sterile package that was big enough to cover the entire mess on his back. I brought everything to the bedside and dumped them on the end of the bed.

In the third kit, I found a tube of liquid bandage and handed it to Troy. He had taken out all the rough sutures I put in. He snatched the tube and opened it, tracing the I with the skin glue. He waited a few moments for the glue to dry and then he took the bandage in the sterile package and opened it. Only the edges were sticky and he gently covered the wound so none of the sides touched the cut.

The garbage bucket next to him was full of the kind of waste that would stink in a few hours. I would need to throw it in the incinerator as soon as we were done here. He set out three containers of antibiotics, with three needles, on the nightstand next to me.

"Every three hours." He pointed and then headed into the bathroom to wash up his hands.

I nodded and straightened up the bed. Mikhail watched me.

"I'm going to throw this stuff down the incinerator downstairs. I'll be back."

"Then we can talk," he said with a goofy smile.

"You're high."

"Mhmmm."

"I can take that stuff down," Troy said as he came out of the bathroom.

"He can take that stuff down," Mikhail mimicked.

"I appreciate the offer. But I need to grab my clothes from down there anyway and get them in the washing machine, so I don't have to trounce around in a dress."

"I'm going to try to get a little more sleep until daybreak at least," Troy said. "Then we need to start putting together a strategy for transporting the rest of that bleach."

"I'll be down."

"You need to administer his medicine." He pointed at the neatly lined up row of medicine. "We can talk strategies later."

"Okay." I picked up the garbage can. "I'll be right back," I said to Mikhail as we left the room together.

I punched in the code without caring whether Troy saw it or not. I was tired and frazzled and really, I was avoiding Mikhail. I wasn't ready to talk about my dream. Not with all the ramifications.

Troy walked silently next to me, and he was the one who opened the door to the operating room, holding it open for me. I dumped the contents of the garbage can down the incinerator shoot and went to the scrub room to find my clothes.

I pulled them off the hooks and turned to leave. Troy leaned against the door, blocking my way out.

"Can I be blunt?"

My throat closed, forcing my voice to squeak out an answer. The dream surfaced and I couldn't stop the shiver that started at the base of my spine. "Sure."

"What is your relationship with the dragon?"

I stepped back and bit down on the instinctive "None of your business" that wanted to tumble from my lips. "Why?"

"I'm just trying to figure it out."

"He's my… friend." That much I knew. After all we had been through, he was the one I could count on to have my back.

"Just friends?"

The dream flashed in my mind and the way my heart had soared when Mikhail kissed me. I focused on Troy. "He's a dragon. I'm not," I finally said. It wasn't really an answer either, and my stomach squeezed.

Half of his lips formed a smile. "Go tend to your friend. I'll come up in the morning after I get a few more hours of sleep." He turned and sauntered to the door, giving me a full view of his backside clad in tight boxers and what I could be missing.

On the way out of the scrub room, I grabbed a pair of crutches on impulse.

Troy held the door open and turned off the lights before latching the lock behind us. "Don't forget to turn out the lights in the stairwell when you get up there." He headed down as I turned away from the pleasant view and headed up to my naked dragon.

21

Mikhail's eyes were closed when I checked in on him. Instead of just dropping my clothing on the ground and crawling into the bed like I wanted to, I headed to the laundry room and dropped my clothing in the washing machine before I turned out the lights and made my way back to the bedroom.

The light from the library was still in place by the bed, and I was tempted just to leave it, but with my luck I'd trip on it in the middle of the night while I tried to get to the bathroom, so I unplugged it and moved it to the far side of the room. I didn't want to do something that would startle Mikhail into moving when he shouldn't.

I set the bedside alarm for three hours and turned out the light. When I finally settled, facing Mikhail, I glanced at him.

His eyes were open and still held that glossy drugged quality. "Holly?"

There was so much in the way he said my name that the walls slammed into place. I didn't want to be harassed about a dream. A dream I wanted so badly to be true, no less. "Not tonight, Mikhail."

"Yes. Tonight. Because I'm drugged up enough to speak my mind and possibly not remember in the morning."

I sighed and met his serious gaze. "I'm not in the mood for your razzing."

"As tempting as that may be, I'm not going to razz you, but I do have questions. Were you dreaming about me?"

"You already know the answer to that." I went to roll away, but his hand landed on my arm in a soft, but insistent grip.

He smiled timidly, like what he had to say was concerning and yet he had to say it. "Then you are experiencing the same... emotions I am?"

"And what are you experiencing, Mikhail?" I did not want to play this game and my voice held every ounce of exasperation pummeling my muscles.

He gave me a heavy sigh. "At first I thought it was just pure lust. If I hadn't burned you, I probably would have coerced you into bed before we left this apartment." His grip on my arm changed to a soft caress.

His admission caught my full attention. "So, you *did* want to know me in the biblical sense."

"I want to know you in *every* sense. Yes."

I scrunched my eyebrows together as I studied the openness in his gaze. "Then what the hell is with the mixed messages? Why push me toward Troy?"

He huffed. "You asked me that in your dream." He closed his eyes. "I'm toxic, Holly. As much as I want the dream—" He opened his eyes again. "My dream, not yours—I know I'll screw up."

I wasn't quite sure what to do with that confession, so I focused on his earlier words while I digested this new one. "You said at first it was lust. What is it now?"

His hand moved to my cheek. "You really have to ask?" He searched my eyes like he was looking for the answer instead of giving it to me.

"No games. I really need to hear it from you."

"It's more. Respect, adoration... all the things I promised myself I'd never let enter my life again, because the loss that is inevitable will crush me this time."

"It's not inevitable." I put my hand over his. The warmth of him in contrast to the feeling he was pulling away now that he had said his piece made me want to hang onto this puddle he created in my chest.

"You are not immortal. Death is inevitable. It's just a matter of decades at best, hours at worst."

My skin broke out in gooseflesh, and I thought I understood his dilemma. My lips pulled down at the edges, and I pressed them together at the sudden drop of my stomach.

"Love can't overcome death." He rubbed his thumb over my bottom lip. "And if I'm not careful, I could be the cause of your death. I cannot live with that."

A chill skittered up my spine. "What the hell are you talking about? You were married to a human before. What makes *me* so different?"

"*You* can still have children."

My brain raced back to our conversations in the dark subway system after he broke me out of Grand Central. If he got me pregnant, I would die in childbirth. Dragons ate their way out of the egg.

And in a human, the egg was the womb. I closed my eyes as sharp pain gripped my chest.

"So, because of that, you chose not to love me?"

"No. In spite of the danger, in spite of trying to deny it to myself, I've still fallen in love with you." His eyes shone brighter, giving me a view of his sad smile. "And as much as I want you—as much as I love you—I cannot sentence you to such a horrifying death."

I rolled away from him so he wouldn't see the tears that sprouted in my eyes. "Troy asked what you were to me." My voice shook with silent tears.

"And what did you say?" His fingers gently ran through my hair like I had done to him earlier.

"I lied. I told him you were my friend." I closed my mouth on the sob that wanted to escape.

"I am your friend," Mikhail whispered and ran his fingers down my back.

"No, Mik, you're far more than that to me, too. And I can't keep ignoring it."

"Maybe if you get laid, it will clear your head," he said with a lilt in his voice that made me want to smack him.

I turned enough to glare at him.

"Your words, not mine." He grinned like an adolescent fool.

I couldn't believe this ancient being could carry so much wisdom at the same time as so much bullshit. "You're such an evil shit sometimes." I sniffled.

"I am. Especially since I won't remember this, and you will." His eyes sparkled with mischief.

"Evil son of a bitch," I repeated and settled in with my back to him.

A few minutes later, his hand fell onto the bed, and his snore started almost immediately.

I stared at the clock. Tears blurred the numbers and I let them fall as my heart broke. Mikhail would never give in to his feelings. Not if it put me in danger. And damn him, now that I knew what was in his heart, I would never leave his side.

Talk about an impossible situation. We had more chance of taking out all the monsters without an injury than acting on this ache in our chests.

22

The alarm went off every three hours, waking both of us. I administered his antibiotic just as Troy had prescribed. The first two times, Mikhail was still in a drugged stupor, and he just laid his arm out for me to do my thing. Then he folded it back under the pillow and started to snore immediately.

The third time, sunlight brushed the room. And I stretched. All in all, I probably scored ten hours of solid sleep. I needed something to eat after I gave Mikhail his meds. I turned to him, and he stared at me with a creased forehead.

"I hurt everywhere." He lowered his arms to his side.

I gave him his morning dose of penicillin. "You've been in the same position for a little more than a day. I'd imagine you'd be stiff."

"Troy didn't give me morphine, did he?" he asked with his brow creased.

"No. He gave you oxycodone."

Relief washed over Mikhail's face, and he closed his eyes. "Morphine can kill me. Kind of like penicillin can kill you."

I froze in place with the empty needle in my hand. "You're allergic to it?"

"Yes. I told you that last night. At least I think I did. It might have been in the operating room." He rubbed his face. "It fucks with our ability to breathe."

"You should have been clearer about that," I snapped as my heart pounded in my chest. I could have killed him last night had I not thought to grab something else besides the morphine. I took the full vial on my nightstand and tossed it into the trash because I did not want any mistakes, especially because the vials didn't look any different between the penicillin and the morphine. Same size, same shape, and same white label with faded black lettering.

I swallowed hard and tossed the empty needle in the garbage as well. Before I left the bedroom, I ran my finger down the length of his foot.

He jerked it away and looked down at me with irritation in his eyes. "Hey. That tickles."

I stared at him as hope filled my chest. I slowly ran my hand up his calf, massaging as I went.

"That feels good." He closed his eyes.

I don't know what possessed me, but I didn't stop at his knee. I went higher and received a rumble of satisfaction in his throat as I massaged both thighs now.

He feels my hands on him. The thought galloped through me as fast as my heart clanged in my chest. I wasn't sure why I was compelled to continue. Maybe it was that satisfied rumble coming from him or the conversation last night or I don't know what, but I couldn't stop. His warm skin felt like silk under my fingers. His muscles pulled taut and then relaxed as I worked out the kinks.

Even his ass was a wonder to knead. Hell, if he had been on his back, I think his cock would have been as hard as a rock and waiting for satisfaction. I skipped over his lower back for fear that rubbing near the incision would irritate it and set him back again, but his middle back and shoulders were just as much of a playground as the rest of him.

His breathing was low and relaxed, and I stopped after massaging each arm. He turned to look at me, meeting my gaze. The sleepiness slowly cleared, and he looked over his shoulder and bent his left leg and then rolled his ankle around.

"It worked," I barely whispered. "This isn't a dream, is it?"

His gaze popped back to mine. He reached out and pinched my arm.

"Ouch." I swatted him away. I retaliated and he sucked air through his teeth.

"Not dreaming." His gaze lingered on me. "Did you by chance bring me anything to walk with?"

"Crutches." I pointed to the wall near my side of the bed.

"Think you can bring them to me?"

"Should you really be moving?"

He bit his lip and lifted both legs, one at a time and then shrugged. "If I don't, I'm going to soil this bed," he said. "And I don't think I've done that yet."

I got the crutches from where I left them and stepped away as he slowly shifted to push himself into a sitting position. Then he hauled himself up using the crutches and used them like he was an old pro.

The bathroom door shut against my lingering stare.

"No showering yet," I called through the door and then collected all the bloody towels, throwing them into the garbage. I also stripped the comforter and took that to wash, transferring my clothes to the dryer before I shoved the comforter into the washing machine and started it on a large load.

When I came back into the bedroom, Mikhail had already slipped on a pair of sweatpants and sat on the side of the bed. Thankfully, none of the mess slipped through the towels to stain the sheets. I didn't think it made it to the comforter either, but I wanted it clean just in case.

I used the moment to slip into the bathroom, relieve myself, and polish my teeth and to avoid the overwhelming feelings tightening my stomach.

His brow was creased, and he hadn't moved from where he sat when I came back into the room.

"We talked, didn't we." It wasn't really framed as a question and his eyes searched out mine.

I stayed just out of arm's reach and nodded.

His eyes narrowed as he stared at the wood floor under my feet. "It's all... fuzzy."

I couldn't do this. I couldn't pretend I didn't want him, and he didn't want me. I started out of the room, and he had enough of a reach to grab my wrist and pull me to the spot in front of him.

"What did I say?" His eyes searched mine and then they closed.

"I'll get out of your hair." I broke his grip on my wrist, turned, and walked out of the bedroom, straight to the door. I couldn't be by his side in the light of day. Not knowing that he was purposely ignoring his feelings.

The squeak of the crutches followed and before I could get the entire code in, he pushed me against the door, his breath heaving from the exertion of moving that fast.

"Don't..."

"Don't what?" I spun, facing him. He was close enough to smell the sweet freshness of his clean breath.

"I—" He stopped and dropped his head. "Don't go."

"Why should I stay if you are going to deny both of us the possibility of real joy? Do you know how rare that is?"

He growled, actually growled at me, and then both crutches fell to the floor. He took my face in his hands and crushed my lips with his. It wasn't the sweet kiss from the dream, but it was a damn fine start.

I pinched him again.

"Ouch. What was that for?" He pulled away to look me in the eye.

"Just making sure."

A slow smile appeared. "That dream really fucked with your head, didn't it?" He pinched me, and then resumed the kiss despite my whine. "This is real," he whispered against my lips. "And it will be the death of me," he added. And then his mouth demanded more, his tongue searched, teased, played with mine until he nearly lost his balance, reminding both of us of his less-than-optimal health.

I slowly pushed him away and reached down, picking up one crutch and the next before I stood up. "You need these. Otherwise, we're going to end up on the floor."

"Maybe that was my intention." His eyes sparkled bright.

As much as I wanted that, I knew it would strip him of all his strength and could do some damage to whatever healing had already taken place. "Nourishment before we deplete you of all your reserves." I slid out of the space between him and the door and headed into the kitchen.

He took a seat on the other side of the counter, watching my every move.

"Stop staring. You're making me self-conscious."

His smile slowly faded. "Holly?"

I looked up at him.

"We can't take our focus off the goal," he said softly, like it was going to set me off.

I sighed and met his gaze. "No. I suppose we can't do that. This…" I waved my finger between the two of us. "This will have to wait until we've done our job."

He bit his lower lip for a few minutes while I cracked eggs into a bowl. "It is something to look forward to." He met my gaze. Then a smile formed again, like a ray of sun breaking through storm clouds.

God, he was a gorgeous man when he smiled like that. His citrine eyes lit up like fireworks when his smile reached them. I couldn't think of a better way to reward ourselves if we were successful. "Another driving motivation for both of us." I grinned back.

He sighed and shifted on the chair as his gaze traveled over me like a soft caress. The gentleman in him wouldn't say what was behind that look.

"Until then, I'll just rely on my dreams," I said with a wicked smile.

His cheeks turned a pleasant shade of pink. "I can assure you, I'm much better in real life than a dream."

Before I was able to form any sort of verbal reply, a knock on the door interrupted our teasing.

"Troy," we both said at the same time as reality yet again crashed into us.

I set the bowl of eggs I had been whipping down on the counter and crossed to the door, swinging it open.

Troy carried two cups of coffee in his hands, and he stepped inside, handing me a cup. "I didn't see a coffee machine when I was here earlier and figured you might need one." His glance landed on Mikhail sitting at the counter and his eyebrow cocked. "You're looking better than the last time I saw you."

"Yes. The antibiotics every three hours was a smart call. It helped a great deal."

I pointed at Mikhail. "You still need one more dose." Then I glanced at Troy. "Do you want some scrambled eggs?" I pointed at the mixture in process.

"Thanks, but I ate with the guys. They are enjoying the accommodations, but we can't let ourselves become too complacent." He glanced at Mikhail. "I can grab you a coffee if you'd like." He pointed toward the door.

Mikhail took a sip of his orange juice and shrugged. "I don't drink coffee, but thanks for the offer."

"Did you talk strategy?" I asked as I poured the eggs into the pan. The sizzle filled the space.

"Not yet. We need to be in top shape before we go out. Tiredness breeds mistakes. Another good night of rest and a day of nutrition, and we'll be ready to go."

That made perfect sense to me, and I focused on not burning our breakfast.

"I should check your bandages," he said to Mikhail and waved toward the bedroom.

They left me to finish cooking the meal. A dangerous endeavor in itself, but I managed not to burn the eggs and the toast came out golden brown. Not one error in the breakfast department. I buttered the toast and set them on each of the plates. I put salt and pepper on the counter and a couple of forks.

They still hadn't come out yet. I placed the plates on the counter and crossed to the bedroom as worry replaced the growl in my stomach.

"Breakfast is going to get cold." I pushed the door wide open.

Mikhail hiked up his sweatpants and glanced at me over his shoulder.

His eyes conveyed more than Troy's, and Troy's held enough concern for me to swallow hard.

"What's wrong?"

"His leg looks better, but there are still signs of infection with his back. So, I want another twenty-four hours of antibiotics. One vial every three hours."

"I… um. I don't know if there is that much left."

Troy met my gaze and then seemed to digest my words. "After you eat, we can go check to see how many there are. If there isn't enough, I'll figure out the dosage you need to spread it out over that period."

With a clean patch on his back, Mikhail crutched into the living room and took a seat in front of his plate.

"Are you sure?" I asked Troy before we followed.

"The red lines have diminished, but they are not all gone."

I took a deep breath and nodded. I needed food before I ventured back down to the medical facilities.

"There isn't anywhere else you keep medicine like that, is there?" I asked and then took a bite of my breakfast.

"No. I thought I had enough stocked away. I guess I never entertained the thought it would be for me." Mikhail dug into his food without saying more until he cleared his plate. "I can go down with you."

"No. You need to rest. I don't want you exerting yourself. Especially if there isn't enough antibiotics. Overexertion will set you back." Troy didn't give any leeway in his answer.

"Yes, sir," Mikhail said, although he was not happy about it.

I started to do the dishes.

"I can do that. You go with the sergeant to see what's left." He crutched around into the kitchen and moved aside so I could slip out. He didn't offer me any assurances either, and I couldn't help but think maybe we were doomed.

Doomed by our situation.

Doomed by the monsters.

Doomed by fate.

I gave Mikhail one last glance and headed down the stairwell for the umpteenth time in the last twenty-four hours.

23

When we stepped into the operating room, Troy took my arm and turned me to him. "Can he do what you say he can do?"

Another dream déjà vu. I blinked up at him and practically recited word for word what I had in the dream. "Yes. Just look at this building. He's made it functional on its own grid and disguised it to the outside world. Both human and monster from the street level think this is one of the destroyed buildings. If he can do that, a bomb ought to be a snap."

Troy kept his hand around my upper arm. "I don't doubt that he can build it. I think any of us in this building right now has the capability of doing that. It's the delivery of it that has me concerned." He took a breath. "If it's not done at the precise height and velocity, it will only injure a fraction of their army. And how do we get them all in one place to begin with?"

Damn, he was sharp. I stared up into his blue eyes. "We hadn't gotten that far in the plan." I knew Mikhail pondered the delivery system, but I don't think he got far enough to have a detailed plan of attack. Or if he did, he hadn't shared it with me yet.

"What else is in this building?"

Neither of us had had time to explore. "Labs. At least that is what he hinted at before. But I don't know." I glanced at his grip on my arm. His hand was warm and solid, and it unnerved me. "We need to find out how many vials of antibiotics are left." I reminded him of our initial purpose for visiting this room again.

He looked at his hand still gripping me. "Oh. Sorry." He let go before he stepped back giving me some room.

I started toward the medicine closet.

"What if he's just bullshitting us?" he asked. "What if all this is part of the game?"

I paused with my hand on the cabinet and glanced at him. He stood with his hands on his hips and his head bent so he was studying the floor. His concerns were ones I had been working my way through since I was dragged out of Grand Central weeks ago.

I crossed back to him and tilted his chin up so he would meet my gaze. "I went through the same thought process as you are going through. I doubted his motives. If he truly wanted to do us harm, he would have let us perish in that bomb at City Hall. He didn't have to save any of us."

"He did it to save you." He pressed his finger against the bare skin above my breasts and he didn't remove it right away.

Silence settled between us, his gaze intense and sharp. His hand settled onto my skin, right over my heart.

My heart that was beating like a sparrow caught in a trap. His eyes dropped to the connection of our skin. Then he licked his lips and slowly pulled his hand away as if he just crossed a line he knew he shouldn't have.

My libido balked, but my heart sighed with relief. Too much of the dream had already been laid bare in real life and I couldn't fathom the ramifications if he were to go further.

I turned back toward the medical cabinet when Troy muttered, "Fuck it."

He spun me around and planted a kiss, pushing me against the medicine cabinet. One of his hands landed between my legs and the other on my breast as his tongue swiped across my lips. And damned if he knew the spots to rub just right.

I opened my mouth, and instead of arguing, I let my tongue play with his as his hands worked a physical magic that set my body tingling. When he started pulling my dress up, I pushed him back.

"We... um..." I wiped my face, trying to put my thoughts together, but the bulge in the front of his pants made that difficult. It had literally been over a year since I'd had the opportunity to get laid. And although my heart was all in with Mikhail, I really needed this to be able to focus on what we needed to do. But I was sure if Mikhail found out, he'd have one hell of a hissy fit.

"Don't read too much into it, Woods. I just..."

I stared at his hungry blue eyes. "Need to get laid," I finished his sentence as the need took over my entire being. I moved toward him.

Before I could blink, he had me in his arms and kissed me hard enough to yank the air from my lungs. My hands found his belt and fumbled with it as he moved me to the tabletop and pushed my dress up around my waist. In the next instant, his entire length was inside me.

We moved like frantic teenagers. His mouth on mine, plundering as his hands gripped my thighs, moving me with such force my breath exhaled hard with every thrust of his hips. It was fast and hot and when it was over, we were both panting like animals.

He held me in place as the last of the tremors gripped him. I dropped back on the table trying to catch my breath. Guilt bit at the edges of my mind, but my body was totally satiated. At least now I wouldn't obsess over Mikhail so much and my focus could be on killing the monsters.

Troy smiled an exhausted smile. "I'm sorry, Woods, but I've been wanting to do that for a while." He pulled out and stumbled back as he zipped himself up. He hand-combed his hair and turned back toward the medical cabinet.

"I'll be right back." I headed into the scrub room and the bathroom stall just beyond the showers. I relieved myself and then cleaned up as best I could with a wet washcloth. My cheeks were still rosy from the exertion and my hair was a mess. I tried to tame it into submission, but that wasn't working, so I dampened my hand and used water to get it in order.

I came out. Troy had four vials on the table, and he was chewing his lower lip. I wasn't sure whether it was because we were short the medicine or he was reflecting on what had just happened.

"Is that all there is?" I went to the cabinet to rifle around just in case we missed something. I slammed the cabinet closed and looked around, hell-bent on ignoring the elephant in the room.

"I already looked in the logical places while you were cleaning up." Troy met my gaze. "We might need to make a medical run."

His statement pulled the air from my lungs, and I slumped on the cabinet. Medical runs were more dangerous than the bleach recovery was. At least that had a known path, a known destination, and a known stash. Medical runs were usually a bust. Most pharmacies were barren, and hospitals were worse. They were usually crumbling structures like the one Mikhail had gone into before we got to my platoon.

I guess my face reflected the near panic that sent my heart into my throat because Troy said, "Before you get all worried about your friend and shit, let's see if this clears it up. I'll be back before nightfall to check on him."

I didn't correct his reference of Mikhail as my friend. Somehow, I knew all this would bite me. I just didn't know when.

Troy came over and put the vials in my hand, closing his around mine. "He isn't just your friend, is he?"

I blinked up at him, taking the medicine. "No. It's... complicated."

He inhaled and raised an eyebrow. "So, you'd prefer if I kept this quiet."

I stared up at him and nodded. "I needed an itch scratched," I said, almost cringing at how crude I sounded.

"That makes two of us," he said. "But when all this is over, and the monsters are gone, and the world awakens, the three of us are going to have to have a coming to Jesus on the subject."

I blinked and my mouth ran dry.

Troy looked down at my hands. "After his next full dose, give him half doses every three hours." He added eight syringes to the pile in my hand, and then led me to the door and sent me up the stairs.

My brain was still reconciling his words when I got to the penthouse door. I balanced my stack of meds and punched in the code. Mikhail was in the chair, reading a book, with his leg on the ottoman as I entered the room.

I didn't say anything. I just crossed to the bedroom before the jars in my arms fell and broke. I organized them and then looked at the clock. We still had a good half hour before his next dose.

When I stepped into the living room, Mikhail's stare pierced through me. His irises blazed and his jaw muscle jumped.

"There were only four vials," I said, but I couldn't quite meet his gaze.

He silently stared at me and slammed the book closed, making me jump. "You do know a dragon's sense of smell is at least a hundred times that of humans, right?"

I pressed my lips together, sucking my lower one between my teeth as my brain wrapped around his words. *Could he smell...* I looked up at him, at the glare in his eyes. *Oh, God. He could smell that I had sex.*

His eyes narrowed to slits. "What kind of game are you really playing?"

"I don't play games." But my words sounded meek, even to my ears.

"Bullshit!" He heaved the book across the room. "I bare my soul to you, and you fuck someone else?" Smoke curled from his nostrils.

"I didn't intend to." It sounded like such a weak argument, and I expected him to turn me to ash at any moment.

"Did he force himself on you?" He growled the words.

I looked down at my hands and back up at him, shaking my head. "No."

Hurt flashed for a moment and then his eyes turned to steel. "Why?"

"Because I cannot focus with this much sexual tension. It diminishes my ability to think. And we need to focus on what we need to do," I snapped. "Basically, you're making me crazy."

"You're blaming your lapse of judgment on me?" He stood and grabbed a crutch. "Fuck you, Woods!" He headed toward the bedroom with smoke billowing out of his nostrils.

I intercepted him, blocking his retreat despite the warning signs. He could toast me at any moment, but I didn't care. I needed to make this right. "You're the one who keeps pulling away."

He leveled a smoke-filled glare. "I wasn't the one who pulled away this morning."

I took a deep breath. "True, but then you hammered the point home. This wasn't something we could focus on right now."

"I did not say that. You did."

"You said we had to focus on the goal."

He pressed his lips together and his entire face turned red. "Own your shit, Holly. Don't put the blame on me for this one."

I blinked at his furious glare. "I'm human. I am prone to fucking up things."

"And you certainly fucked this up." He pushed past me and slammed the door.

I leaned my forehead on the door as my throat tightened. This was the polar opposite of the dream. I royally screwed myself. "Mikhail?"

Silence. But I could see his shadow against the door. I swallowed hard.

"I'm sorry. I wasn't thinking at all," I whispered. "He made a move because he assumed we were friends and I... I was selfish."

"You don't have the foggiest idea what love is," he said with a voice full of bitterness.

I sighed. "You're right. Every time I've let someone in, they've crushed me in the same callous, thoughtless way." My history with men even before the pandemic was a repeat of today, except the other way around. I bared my soul, and they fucked my best friend.

The alarm went off in the bedroom. "You need to let me in so I can give you your shot," I said, hoping he wouldn't sabotage his progress.

His shadow didn't move and the alarm shut off with a bang as if he heaved something at it. "I trusted you," he finally said.

"I know."

"With my life."

Tears blurred my eyes. I covered my mouth, but a sob escaped between my fingers. He was right. I needed to own my shit. There was no valid reason to break his trust. I slid down to the floor and put my head on my knees, letting the tears flow.

The bedroom door opened, and he took a seat next to me and leaned against the door jamb. He didn't touch me, and he didn't speak. When I finally looked up at him, his expression was unreadable.

"I knew you'd be the death of me," he whispered and ran his hands through his hair.

"I'm sorry." My voice hitched through the words.

"I will turn him to ash if he gets near you again."

I just nodded and climbed to my feet. I crossed and grabbed the last vial that I had brought from last night and one of the needles. When I came back to his side, he held out his arm and looked away. I gave him the shot and ran my finger down his arm near where I pricked him.

He yanked his arm away with a feral growl.

I opened my mouth to ask him whether he'd ever forgive me or whether I had done irreparable harm to what had actually started. But before I could form words, he interjected.

"Do not even think about asking if I'll ever forgive you. Now is not the time. And just so you understand the ramifications of your actions, it will be a cold day in hell before I touch you again." His eyes blazed. "You can sleep on the couch. And do not touch my wife's things again. Understand?"

I leaned back, accepting his vitriol. I deserved every ounce of it, and I'd take it until he was physically better. I glanced at the line of penicillin. "Where is the nearest drug store?" I brought my gaze back to him.

He blinked at me, narrowing his eyes. "What?"

"That is the last of the penicillin." I pointed at the vials. "I need to know where the nearest drug store is."

He studied my face and then looked at the four vials on the nightstand. Something flashed across his face, and he shook his head. "I'm not letting you go on a suicide mission."

"You don't have a say in the matter."

He grabbed my throat and brought me within an inch of his face. "I have the only say," he growled. Smoke drifted from his nostrils and his irises were fully engulfed in flame. "My terms are the only terms, or I will turn this entire building into ash and let the leviathans tear me to pieces."

He let me go with a shove.

I fell back on my ass and glared at him as I rubbed my throat, shocked at his behavior. It lit the stubbornness inside me as well as indignation. I stood and stripped off the dress, throwing it on his lap, and marched away before the tears started again. My clothes had long dried in the dryer and I put them on before I moved the comforter to the dryer.

I crossed into his study and slammed the door. But before I threw myself on the couch, I glanced at the clock, calculating when Mikhail's next dose would be.

I wanted to smash everything in the room.

I wanted to curse Mikhail to hell.

And I desperately wanted to turn back the clock and stop myself from making this catastrophic mistake.

24

I emerged from the den nearly three hours later, ignored Mikhail lounging on the couch, and used the bathroom. The comforter was dry, so I carried it to the bedroom and dumped it on the bed before grabbing his next dose of medicine. I only filled the needle halfway and then went out to the couch.

He stared at me as I tapped the needle before stabbing it in his arm and depressing the plunger. His gaze lowered to his arm and his head tilted as he looked back at me.

"Holly?" He put his hand on his chest. His breath wheezed.

I looked at the needle and my eyes widened. *What the hell had I grabbed? I threw the morphine away, hadn't I?* I dropped the syringe and bolted into the bedroom with my heart pounding and my throat tight enough to make me gasp. I flipped on the nightstand light.

I picked up the vial and my finger moved the label. Although the top one said penicillin, the bottom one had morphine stamped in that faded black lettering. "No, no, no, no." I repeated the words and looked at the next and the next and the next, pushing the fake labels away from each one. That bastard gave me morphine vials, not penicillin, knowing Mikhail was allergic.

"No!" I screamed and ran into the living room. Mikhail didn't need to turn Troy to dust when he saw him. I was going to cut out his heart with a spoon. "No, no, no. Mikhail. Please don't leave me."

His breath came in alarming hisses like he wasn't getting enough oxygen and I straddled him.

"Now's not the time," his voice labored.

"The bastard gave me morphine, not penicillin." I pulled Mikhail up and onto his feet. "Walk with me, keep moving, maybe you can burn this shit off with your dragon metabolism." I nearly dragged him from one end of the apartment to the other, alternating between panicking and seething.

"Nasal spray in medicine cabinet." His breathing was shallow now.

I didn't even doubt him. I moved with him into the bathroom and swung open the cabinet. He raised his hand, pointing to something behind his shaving cream.

I pulled it out of the cabinet.

"Bed," he whispered.

I pulled him into the bedroom and laid him down and then read the instructions. Why Mikhail had an antidote to an allergic reaction to morphine in his bathroom I didn't want to know, but I was so thankful he did. I shoved it into his nose and depressed, then followed with his other nostril.

"I'm going to kill that bastard," I whispered as I re-read the directions.

Mikhail grabbed my arm. "Again." This time his voice wasn't as labored.

I plunged the nasal spray into each nostril again. Waited a moment and then did it a third time, which emptied the rest of the antidote into his system. I lay my ear on his chest, listening to his lungs struggle.

"Please, please don't die. I'm an idiot. An idiot who is in love with your dragon ass and possibly the stupidest human who ever walked the planet.

Please, please, please don't die on me. Not now." The mantra continued.

So did his heartbeat. After a while, his breathing evened out.

And after an even longer while, his arms engulfed me. I sobbed on his chest. Harder than I had at the door. Mikhail held me and kept breathing long, slow, steady pulls.

"I'm okay," he finally said with a slur.

I shook my head, not accepting his placation. "I could have killed you." My voice shook. I looked up. "I almost did." My chin trembled. "If you didn't have that in the medicine cabinet…"

"Any time I give someone morphine, I stock my cabinet." He met my gaze. "You're the reason I had it." He brushed my hair from my face. "A little bit of serendipity there."

I let out a near hysterical laugh that ended in tears again. Finally, when the well of tears dried, I sat up and wiped my face. "Do you own a handgun?"

He shook his head. "But I do have an ancient katana in the study on top of the bookshelves."

"Are you out of danger?" I did not want to leave his side if he might have a relapse.

He nodded.

I stood and swiped all the bottles off the nightstand. "He is mine." I leveled a glare and then marched out to the living room and lined up the vials on the kitchen table within view of the door, breaking all the fake label seals, and placed the needle in front of the display before I went into the den. I had missed this gem before, but that's because it wasn't displayed like it should have been. It was nearly hidden.

I climbed up the shelves and grabbed it off the top, admiring the beautifully ornate sheath. I removed the blade and marveled at the perfect steel. It was sharp enough to draw blood when I ran the edge of my thumb along the blade.

That would do. That would do just fine.

I grabbed it and then unlocked the door, cracking it before I took a seat in the corner chair in the shadows with only the light from the laundry room on, illuminating the vials on the table.

I laid the blade across my lap and waited.

I did not care what Troy's reasoning was for what he did. He was going to die tonight by my hand.

25

Another couple of hours went by before the door creaked open. Troy silently closed the door behind him. His gaze landed on the vials lined up and the empty needle laid in front of the display. He reached for the door, but I had engaged the lock code so the moment it closed, the lock engaged.

"You killed him," I said, making my voice low and menacing.

He stiffened and turned, scanning the apartment until his gaze landed on me.

"Was fucking me part of the plan?" I cocked my head. He hadn't yet seen the blade in my lap. I had to be careful. He was military and despite my black belt that I earned before the world went to hell, I was sure he, as an elite soldier, had many more moves than I had. So, my best bet was a surprise attack.

"No. Blood poisoning is a painful way to die. Morphine overdose isn't."

I narrowed my eyes. "Are you telling me you were honestly trying to be humane?"

"There wasn't any more penicillin." He took a step closer.

We had gotten sidetracked before I could open the cabinet, but I had been certain there had been more the last time I grabbed some, just not certain that there were eight left. "Did you know there wasn't any left when we went down there?"

He looked at the floor and then up at me.

"You took them."

"My first priority is to my team."

My hand gripped the blade harder. "So, again, that advance was what, a diversion so you had the opportunity to poison Mikhail?"

He pressed his lips together and his open expression morphed to a glare. "He was a dragon," he hissed. "A filthy fucking dragon."

"Then why fix him up? Why amputate his leg and fix the issues with his back incision?"

He shrugged. "Medic training. And there was no way you'd let him die. But it ultimately gave me the opportunity I was looking for since we set foot in that subway tunnel."

I refrained from jumping up and charging. There were still too many steps between us. I just glared at him. "So, you used me."

"Yes. I screwed with your mind and scratched my own itch. Plus, fucking the dragon's mate— well, that was an added bonus and a big middle finger to the bastard." He stepped closer. "You didn't seem to mind, though."

I remained silent.

"Now *we* can get it on any time *we* feel the need."

"We?"

"Considering you're a traitor to the human race, my team and I have earned liberties whenever the fuck we want." He slipped something over his fingers. Brass knuckles caught in the light. "If you put up a fight, I'll knock you into tomorrow." He held up his hand to show me his new jewelry and stepped within my striking distance.

I stood and spun, aiming for his displayed wrist. It was easier than slicing butter and his hand flew into the side of the couch.

Troy blinked and stared at the stump of his arm as blood shot out of his veins. He screamed and gripped his wrist as I moved back into my next defensive form again.

"Bullshit." This time I lunged into a fencing move and plunged the tip of the blade right into his junk. With a flick of my wrist, I drove the blade across, slicing through whatever I had skewered, and then I retreated a couple of steps, with the blade dripping blood.

His scream went silent, his face turning nearly purple as he fell to his knees. Just as his breath hitched, I spun, releasing a scream of fury that drowned out his high-pitched wail. I sliced through the air with everything I had. The blade hardly caught as it sliced through skin, bone, and sinew, and the bastard's head rolled across the floor. I kicked his headless body backward and stood, huffing with the wrath shaking my entire body.

"Damn, woman."

I looked up at Mikhail in the doorway, leaning on a crutch as he watched me slice up the asshole who compromised me and nearly killed him.

I ran my hand through my hair. My breath still came in heavy pulls. I had never killed a human before. It did not satiate the wrath coiling inside me, either. I wanted to slaughter them all because those bastards on the fifteenth floor were in on this sick plot.

"Excuse me while I go slaughter some more pigs."

"There are four of them, Holly. And you won't have the element of surprise."

I glanced at him, and a new thought dawned on me. One that chilled the fury a few notches. This bastard was alone with Mikhail before we went for the medicine. I dropped the sword on the floor and crossed to him, unconcerned that I was covered in blood. I'd wash it off. I turned Mikhail around and pulled up the shirt he had put on earlier and ripped the bandage off his back.

There were lines traversing out from the incision, but it still looked better than last night. I pulled him back into the bedroom and reached into the box I had brought the other night to grab the second container of dragon blood.

"Shower, now."

"Holly—" he started to argue.

"I don't know what he put on you." I met his gaze. "I administered the antibiotics, but who the hell knows what he's done to make sure you suffer before I gave you an overdose."

I pushed him toward the bathroom. "Strip," I ordered and then turned on the shower. I followed my own orders and stepped in before he did. The water ran red, and I made sure my hands were clean before I soaped up a hand towel.

I moved Mikhail into the spray and gently washed his back from his shoulders all the way down to his ass. The liquid bandage held well enough on the cut I did to his back.

I reached into the bathroom, grabbed the small bench, and put it under the water stream. "Sit."

He did, and I washed his chest, his stomach, his privates, and his legs, ignoring the fact that I was obviously turning him on. I stopped at the bandage around his stump. I handed him the washcloth and then unwrapped the bindings. It didn't look as angry as it had last night, and I gently washed him and then turned the shower off.

"Stay." I reached for a towel and the dragon blood. I dropped to my knees in front of him and took the dry fabric and blotted his leg dry before I handed the bath towel to Mikhail. He put it over his lap, covering his reaction to me.

I took two fingers full of dragon blood and spread it over his stump. This elixir made it so he could walk again. I doubted that it was what caused the blood poisoning. That probably had to do with the non-sterile environment of his bedroom and my inexperience at wielding a scalpel.

I hated to admit that Troy had done an exemplary job at amputation. I glanced up at Mikhail and a horrifying thought dawned. "Did you really need to have this leg removed?"

He touched my cheek gently. "Yes. That would have killed me had he not done it."

"None of this makes any sense." I left the shower to retrieve more bandages for his leg, and I covered his stump in the same manner as it had been. Then I made him stand and turn again while I traced the cut with dragon blood and covered it.

He stood with his back to me, holding onto the shower walls for balance.

"I heard what he said."

"Yeah, well, I was stupid. He did such a good job on you medically, I never suspected he would double-cross you. I didn't realize how deep his hatred was. I underestimated him."

"You weren't the only one." He glanced over his shoulder at me as he wrapped the towel around his waist. "You still have blood in your hair." He hopped out of the shower on his left leg while holding onto the walls.

I moved the bench outside the shower for him and then turned the water back on. I scrubbed my skin and washed my hair three times before the water finally ran clear. When I turned the water off, he handed me a dry towel. I cleaned off and stepped out, scanning the bathroom.

Scanning the carnage.

"I made a hell of a mess of your apartment, haven't I?"

"You've made a hell of a mess of my life." Mikhail looked at the blood-streaked floor and then up at me. "But I can live with that."

"I still have to take care of the others."

"While I appreciate you going all *Kill Bill* out there, I don't want you going alone to address the problem." He pulled me in front of where he sat, and the reference pulled enough of a smile to his lips for me to sigh.

"You can't climb down fifteen flights, Mikhail."

"Yes, I can. I've got crutches."

"Like that is real stealth." I rolled my eyes at him.

"No, I suppose it isn't, but you could carry me." He gave me a smile. "The last time they saw me, I was in mini-dragon form. If you strap that sheath on your back and I play dead..."

He held both my hands in his, gently rubbing the backsides with his thumbs, and I glanced down at the embrace.

"I thought it would be a cold day in hell before you touched me?"

"I thought you had betrayed me but I don't think you really had a choice whether you realize it or not."

I started to pull my hands away, because he was wrong. The choice had actually been mine, not Troy's. I could have left it at pushing him away.

Mikhail clamped down. "He orchestrated it."

"I could have stopped it, but I didn't." I met his gaze. "I'm owning my mistake. Don't water it down."

He nodded but still kept my hands in his. "At first, when that drug hit me, I thought you had done it on purpose. Then I saw your reaction and I wondered how the hell I could have ever doubted you."

My throat tightened. "I really do love you, Mikhail. Which isn't easy for me to admit. And I don't expect you to forgive me for what I did."

He stared into the depth of my eyes. "I love that you aren't begging for forgiveness. Although having you on your knees before me in the shower..." His lips cocked into a smile. "A little groveling like that might work."

I let a small laugh escape. "I saw how much you enjoyed that," I admitted. I glanced at my bloody clothing. "I know you said I couldn't touch anything of your wife's." I started and he squeezed my hands. "Any chance you can let me borrow something to wear?" I met his gaze.

He slowly released my hands. "Grab a pair of jeans and a t-shirt." He nodded toward the bedroom.

I headed to the closet.

"And bring me a pair of sweatpants," he called from the seat in the bathroom.

I still felt as though I walked in slow motion, as if this were a dream, but I knew it wasn't. Still, I pinched my arm to be sure. Pain filtered from the point of the sharp pinch. *Not a dream*. I took a deep breath and the smell of death filtered in from the living room like a reminder of the mess I'd have to clean up later.

I glanced in that direction and the blood pooling slowly across the floor toward the kitchen. I refocused on the closet and pulled a pair of jeans from his wife's side of the closet and then moved the door, so I had Mikhail's side. I didn't want one of his wife's T-shirts constricting my movement, so that left Mikhail's. I debated on which one of his to take and opted for a gray one that seemed more worn than the others. I loved the blue and the green ones on him too much to ruin them, and I was certain that whatever I did would ruin the clothing I wore.

After all, killing was messy. And that was exactly what I intended to do.

I grabbed a pair of sweatpants off the hook on his side and headed back to the bathroom.

Mikhail looked more like himself than he had since I found him pinned under the debris. I crossed to him and stood with the pants in my hand. Contemplating killing the men downstairs somehow made me feel unclean.

Troy had been a different situation; he had actively tried to kill Mikhail and deserved death.

"I have a better idea than walking in with me in your arms. We can stop on twenty-nine and I can cut the building's power in the stairwell and on the floors below," Mikhail said slowly, as if working through an alternative plan in his mind.

"I won't be able to see anything."

"Not necessarily. I might have a night scope or two down there. And I can just walk in and toast them in one blast."

A night scope or two? Man, I needed to see what other goodies this building held. But right now, his idea bloomed too many problems in my head. I handed him the pants as I mentally poked holes in his idea and then in the original plan. Neither of them held tight.

Mikhail pulled the pants on under the towel, seeming more modest now that we had admitted our feelings to each other.

And the more I thought about dropping us all into the dark, the more it disrupted the element of surprise. "They have flashlights, and the bleach is down there, so toasting them could destroy our fuel for the weapon against the leviathan army." That itch of doubt in Mikhail cropped up, but his slow nod and scowl of understanding wiped that out of my mind. "Besides, if the power goes out, they'll know something is wrong. And they do have guns."

He took a deep breath, still nodding. "You're right. I can't just torch the floor. We need that bleach." He closed his eyes with a sigh. "What do you suggest?"

My mind flowed over everything Troy had said. There would be only one entry of mine that made sense with all the information I had been given. But Mikhail was not going to like it at all. "Rip my shirt like we were in some sort of a struggle."

Mikhail didn't question me and did as I asked. I assessed my reflection. The jeans wouldn't work if I was to pull off the plan formulating in my head.

"Are you sure there isn't any women's underwear here?" I glanced back at him as I peeled the jeans off.

Mikhail glanced at me as though I spoke Greek. His gaze dropped to my bare legs and his complexion paled a fraction, but he stood and grabbed the crutch. I followed him into the bedroom. He opened the closet and pulled down a box from the top shelf and held it out for me with dread painted in his eyes.

Inside were little lacy thongs that were definitely not my style, but it would be a hell of a lot better than fighting nude from the waist down. I grabbed a black pair and slipped them on. Again, it was scary how much his wife and I were similarly built.

"I don't like this." He eyed me with deep worry creases in his forehead.

With a deep breath, I launched into the plan formulating in my head. "You need to stay in the shadows of the dark stairwell and hold a handful of my hair while you tell them to have at me. You need to tell them you need to go get rid of the body and you'll be back to have another go."

Mikhail's gaze hardened and his shoulders went rigid. "I'd rather lose the bleach we have than lose you, and this is primed for something bad to happen."

"I will have the sword behind my back. Besides, with the way I'll be standing, they'll think my hands are tied behind my back until it's too late."

He shook his head slowly at me. "No."

"Do you trust me?" The doubt that passed over his features burned but he was right. Trusting me with what I did was a stretch for him right now. "Let me rephrase. Do you trust my abilities with that sword?" I amended, because doubt screamed in his eyes and the set of his frown.

He glanced toward the living room and then nodded despite the displeasure written in the lines around his mouth.

"I need you to try to sound like Troy and say 'Have at her. I've got a body to get rid of.'"

Mikhail repeated the words, but he still sounded like Mikhail. His voice was much deeper than Troy's and very distinct. Although the New York accent worked, the tone needed adjusting.

"You need to make your voice a couple octaves higher."

He tried it again and practically nailed it.

"That was scary perfect." I gave him a smile, but I wasn't sure it convinced him that this would work. "Now the only thing missing is the brass knuckles. If you have them on the hand holding me, where they can see them, it will complete the ruse."

We crossed into the living room, and I tiptoed around the blood, going for the severed hand by the couch. It was harder to get the brass off the stiff fingers than I thought, and I managed to get a couple drops of blood on my leg and all over my hands in the process.

It gave me an idea. I handed the metal to Mikhail and then purposely dragged my hand over the side of my face, as if Troy had clocked me with the metal knuckles. I would never *not* put up a fight and if I showed up all pristine, that would raise a warning.

But I couldn't have blood all over my hands. I picked up the sword and headed into the kitchen, washing off both my hands and the blade.

As I dried my hands with a towel, Mikhail leaned his crutch against the wall and closed his eyes.

His transformation was much quicker than the last time on the operating table. It gave me hope that the antibiotics I had given him worked. He was actually getting stronger by the minute.

With the sword carefully secured in my right hand, I scooped him up, grabbed the crutch, and punched in the code. The stairwell was still lit up and I descended toward a very uncertain future.

26

When we reached the fifteenth-floor landing, I put my ear to the door. I could hear music and talking, like they were having a party in there. I put Mikhail down. His shift back to human form was fast. Almost as fast as his original shift back at Grand Central, which gave me the courage I needed to do what must be done if they indeed were in on Troy's warped plan.

When I handed him the crutch, he looked uncertain, but I gave him a nod. If they were innocent, they would rush to my aid. If they were guilty, they would rush to take advantage of a bound and near naked woman.

Deep down, I prayed they were innocent, but I knew better.

I held the sword so it wouldn't hit me or Mikhail, and he turned the hall lights off, standing in the shadows at my side so he wouldn't get nicked by the sword, and no one would get a clear look at him.

"Ready?" he whispered in my ear, and I nodded. He gently kissed my clean cheek closest to him. "Don't get hurt."

He punched in the code and unlatched the door. With his brass-knuckled hand holding a fistful of hair, he marched me into the room with only part of his arm in view.

My heart dropped at the rigging in the center of the room. It was a mass of chains meant to hold me in whatever position they deemed suitable. My grip tightened on the sword.

"You bastard," I whispered.

"Have at her while I clean up the body."

The door closed behind me, and the four men smiled like hyenas.

"Looks like Troy had a little fun with you before he brought you down."

Juan stayed over by the chains, but Adam, Marvin, and Henry came forward eagerly. Their tented pants announced their intentions as clearly as the hungry looks on their faces.

I widened my eyes, studying them as they approached. They were all about the same height, which gave me an advantage. I had one chance and I turned enough to regrip the sword, faking like I was cowering away from them.

"Bitch isn't such a badass now."

If they actually got close enough to grab me, I was screwed. So, my timing had to be perfect. My heart thundered. When they stepped into range, I twisted, swinging the sword like a baseball bat with a complete follow-through, enough so that I had to pull back before the blade hit my backside.

Nothing happened for a moment. It was as if I had completely missed my targets, but they had stopped in their tracks. Red rings formed on their necks. All at the same height from the floor, but one was closer to the jawline and the others were right smack in the middle of their throats.

Juan stood at the chains, blinking as if he didn't quite understand what had taken place. It wasn't until I kicked Marvin in the chest that Juan's eyes widened into saucers. Marvin's head rolled across the floor toward him.

He stared at it and looked up at me as I stepped into the space the asshole had occupied a moment ago.

I held the dripping blade in front of me and smiled.

Juan turned toward the cots where their bags were located. Where their weapons were. He sprinted. Calculating distance and speed in a millisecond, I launched the sword like a javelin, thankful for the days of track and field in high school. Like my uncanny ability to hit the bull's-eye in any dart match I've ever taken part in, the sword hit Juan just above his ear, stopping when the hilt hit his head. It threw him to the side, where the sword pierced through the front of one of the cabinets.

Juan twitched a few times and then the smell of urine filled the room as his body went slack, hanging from the blade like a sick marionette.

I punched in the code as both Adam and Henry's bodies toppled over.

Mikhail opened the door and surveyed the damage. "Fuck," he said in that long, drawn-out way of his. "Remind me to never get on your bad side."

"I may not be a formally trained soldier, but I've got a black belt and some mad javelin and dart skills. So, yeah. Don't piss me off."

"The true test of your grit is cleanup."

My cockiness faded. "Is the incinerator shaft only on twenty?" I surveyed the damage before me. The thought of dropping the bodies down that dark shaft rolled my stomach.

Mikhail shook his head. "The only place without a garbage shoot is the penthouse."

My gaze landed on the chains they prepared for me. "I killed five men," I said softly and the shakes took hold.

His hand landed gently on my shoulder. "No, Holly. You killed five monsters."

27

Cleaning up reminded me that I was a killer now. No different from Mikhail. I did what I had to do to survive, even though it made me physically ill. He helped however he could, but I didn't want him lifting anything heavy and straining his back. The last thing I wanted was to pop his liquid stitches.

Once everything was cleaned up to the point of being sterilized, I stripped in Mikhail's bathroom again and he gathered all the clothing, tossed it into the washing machine, and dumped nearly an entire bottle of bleach into the water along with detergent.

I balked at the waste, but I secretly hoped it took the blood out of my clothing, especially because that one outfit was all that was truly mine in this place.

We showered again. Diligent about cleaning every drop of blood off our skin. There was nothing sexual about it, and he was quiet and reflective as he washed my body. No words passed between us. But as soon as the drain ran clear, my teeth started to chatter, like I hit a wall of frigid ice and couldn't pull myself free.

I repeated the dragon blood regimen like before and covered his wounds before we dried off. All the while shivering as if we were in a snowstorm with no shelter.

He handed me a nightgown like the one he had lent me when I was healing, and he pulled on boxers and then held the covers up for me to crawl into the bed. I didn't balk or argue. Instead, I slipped under the covers with my back to him, praying that my chills didn't crack a tooth.

It wasn't until Mikhail pulled me against his chest and his warmth wrapped around me that my shivers subsided. Tears began to leak out of the corners of my eyes in a steady stream as the day's events hit like a thousand gnarling leviathans.

He held me as I cried, like he knew the purging of tears was necessary in the face of what amounted to murder. He let me cry without empty platitudes. He let me mourn the loss of some of my own humanity.

When my sobs stopped, he whispered in my ear, "You will be okay, Holly. You're the strongest woman I've ever known."

And yet I was not strong enough to say no to that bastard. That would haunt me for the rest of my days. But perhaps Mikhail was right; he would have coerced me somehow. Although, a part of me didn't believe him. A part of me knew I had lost my moral center over the past week.

I needed the threats to end. I needed a quiet life. And I needed Mikhail to be a part of it, even if that meant hours or days instead of a lifetime.

"Tomorrow, we'll start making bombs," he whispered in my ear just before I let the world drop into the blackness of restless nightmares.

The End

About J.E. Taylor

J.E. Taylor is a USA Today bestselling author, a publisher, an editor, a manuscript formatter, a mother, a wife, a business analyst, and a Supernatural fangirl, not necessarily in that order. She first sat down to seriously write in February of 2007 after her daughter asked:

"Mom, if you could do anything, what would you do?"

From that moment on, she hasn't looked back.

In addition to being co-owner of Novel Concept Publishing, Ms. Taylor also moonlights as a Senior Editor of Allegory E-zine, an online venue for Science Fiction, Fantasy and Horror, and co-host of the popular YouTube talk show Spilling Ink.

She lives in New Hampshire with her husband and during the summer months enjoys her weekends on the shore in southern Maine.

Visit her at www.jetaylor75.com to check out her other titles.

Sign up for her newsletter at https://app.mailerlite.com/webforms/landing/y2z2x6 for early previews of her upcoming books, release announcements, and special opportunities for free swag!